> *"Haven't you ever wondered what might have happened if you'd come back home years ago?"* Travis asked.

"No. No, absolutely not." Eden shook her head vigorously. "I *know* what would have happened here—nothing! My life in Manhattan is no party, but at least it got me away from Edna Rae. She never bothers me there. It's only when I'm in Utah that she comes back to haunt me."

"That's funny," Travis said with the quirk of an eyebrow. "I don't see her anywhere."

"Then look harder, Travis. Edna Rae is right in front of you. Shy and awkward and scared to death."

"Scared? Of me?" Travis grabbed Eden's hand. "Look at me, Eden. The last time we were together, I kissed you. And you kissed me back. I don't know what was going through your head at the time, but judging from your reaction, it sure as blazes wasn't fear!"

Dear Reader,

What better way for Silhouette Romance to celebrate the holiday season than to celebrate the meaning of family....

You'll love the way a confirmed bachelor becomes a FABULOUS FATHER just in time for the holidays in Susan Meier's *Merry Christmas, Daddy*. And in *Mistletoe Bride*, Linda Varner's HOME FOR THE HOLIDAYS miniseries merrily continues. The ugly duckling who becomes a beautiful swan will touch your heart in *Hometown Wedding* by Elizabeth Lane. Doreen Roberts's *A Mom for Christmas* tells the tale of a little girl's holiday wish, and in Patti Standard's *Family of the Year*, one man, one woman and a bunch of adorable kids form an unexpected family. And finally, *Christmas in July* by Leanna Wilson is what a sexy cowboy offers the struggling single mom he wants for his own.

Silhouette Romance novels make the perfect stocking stuffers—or special treats just for yourself. So enjoy all six irresistible books, and most of all, have a very happy holiday season and a very happy New Year!

Melissa Senate
Senior Editor
Silhouette Romance

Please address questions and book requests to:
Silhouette Reader Service
U.S.: 3010 Walden Ave., P.O. Box 1325, Buffalo, NY 14269
Canadian: P.O. Box 609, Fort Erie, Ont. L2A 5X3

HOMETOWN WEDDING

Elizabeth Lane

Silhouette®

ROMANCE™

Published by Silhouette Books

America's Publisher of Contemporary Romance

For My Parents

Author's Note

This story is set in the town where I grew up, and many
of the locations are real. The story and characters,
however, are entirely fictional. No resemblance to
actual persons or events is intended.

 SILHOUETTE BOOKS

ISBN 0-373-19194-4

HOMETOWN WEDDING

Books by Elizabeth Lane

Silhouette Romance

Hometown Wedding #1194

Silhouette Special Edition

Wild Wings, Wild Heart #936

ELIZABETH LANE

has traveled extensively in Latin America, Europe and China, and enjoys bringing these exotic locales to life on the printed page, but she also finds her home state of Utah and other areas of the American West to be fascinating sources for romance, historical and contemporary. Elizabeth loves such diverse activities as hiking and playing the piano, not to mention her latest hobby—belly dancing.

You are cordially invited to attend
the wedding of

Eden Harper
to
Travis Conroy

and

Madge Harper
to
Robert Peterson

on Saturday, the eighth of August

at Our Lady of Mercy Church
at three o'clock p.m.

Reception to follow

R.S.V.P.

Chapter One

He was standing next to the water fountain, one blue-jeaned hip cocked outward as his dark-eyed gaze swept the bustling Salt Lake City air terminal. One hand dangled a dusty Stetson. The other clutched a dog-eared paperback. His long fingers toyed with the book, crushing it, curling it, ruffling its edges in restless impatience.

Eden Harper saw him before he saw her. She had come barreling out of the jetway, intent on making a swift dash across the concourse to the ladies' room, but the sight of him stopped her like a collision with a brick wall.

Travis Conroy.

And he was directly in her path.

Clutching her heavy briefcase, Eden hesitated. She could feel her veneer of Manhattan-bred confidence wilting like a plucked begonia in the midsummer sun. Even after sixteen years, the prospect of bumping into *him* was enough to make her want to crawl back onto the plane and fly wherever it would take her.

She might have been tempted to do just that. Except that for the moment, her feet seemed to be stuck in cement.

She stood gaping like a schoolgirl, her eyes taking in the lanky grace of his six-foot-two-inch height, the crisp, coffee brown curls, the face she had once giddily compared to a sculpted Rodin bronze.

He was older than she remembered—leaner and sharper, the creases sun-bronzed into permanence at the corners of his eyes. But aside from that he looked the same as he had in high school; and as the old humiliation burned through the locked doors of her memory, Eden realized that time had done nothing to heal its caustic sting.

Why Travis Conroy of all people? Why here? Why now?

Even after all these years, he was the last person she ever wanted to see again.

Gathering her wits, Eden turned to slip off in another direction. But no, it was too late. He had spotted her. His eyes flickered in recognition. The hand holding the paperback dropped to his side as the old awkwardness crept over them both.

There was no way out.

Forcing herself to take the offensive, she strode toward him. "Hello!" she exclaimed with a brazen grin. "This is quite a surprise!"

"Yes, it is." His smile was forced, revealing only a flicker of the dimples that had sent girls into rapturous twitters. "Edna, isn't it? Edna Rae Harper?"

As if he could forget.

"It's Eden," she said, trying not to squirm as his eyes took in her beige linen pantsuit and her smartly coiffed pageboy, which had grown considerably blonder with the years. "I, uh, had my name legally changed after I left Monroe."

"Eden." He chewed the name experimentally, like someone tasting sushi for the first time. "I don't recall seeing you down there in quite a while."

His voice was a stranger's, cool and formal. But then, what else could she expect? Sixteen years ago, her little faux pas had been the scandal of South Sevier High School, and Travis Conroy had been its innocent victim. He was probably reliving it right now and grinding his teeth.

"I don't make it home very often," she said, shifting her emotions into neutral. "New York's a long way, even to fly. But my mother's having surgery in a couple of days. I wanted to be with her and to stick around the house until she's on her feet."

"That shouldn't take long. Your mother's a tough lady." He had turned and begun to walk at an ambling pace up the concourse. Feeling awkward and uncertain, Eden moved along beside him. The awful possibility flashed through her mind that somehow he'd been sent here to pick her up—a harebrained idea if ever there was one. The last thing she needed was three hours alone in a vehicle with a man whose presence was a scathing reminder of the worst day of her life.

Whatever he was doing here, she would ride the bus as she'd originally planned. For that matter, she would hike the full 180 miles in her high-heeled sling pumps before she would—

"So, how are you getting home?" he asked cautiously.

One glance at his face confirmed Eden's suspicion that he'd only inquired out of politeness. "The bus," she said. "It's all arranged."

"You're not serious."

"I'm quite serious. Mom isn't up to driving this far to meet my plane, and I can't rent a car because there's no place down there to return it. I'll be taking a cab to the bus depot, and from there—"

"Look," he cut in, his brown eyes crackling with impatience. "The bus doesn't even leave Salt Lake till seven or eight, and it stops at every two-bit town on the road. You won't get home till after midnight. Why don't you—"

"As I said, it's all arranged." Eden turned away with a smile of breezy dismissal and veered for a second set of rest rooms that lay just across the concourse. "Bye," she said, flinging him a last backward glance. "Nice seeing you again."

Bravado still intact, she swung through the rest-room door and collapsed against the wall. Her heart drummed a wild tattoo against her ribs as the fiery blush she'd always hated crept into her cheeks.

This was ridiculous, Eden lectured herself. She was almost thirty years old, and she'd spent the past eight years surviving the jungle world of New York publishing. To be thrown out of kilter by the memory of a silly high-school crush...

But why work herself into a froth? Travis Conroy's reasons for being at the airport obviously had nothing to do with her. All she needed to do was make herself scarce for the next few minutes. By the time she reappeared on the concourse, he was bound to be gone.

The long flight had given her a headache. Fumbling in her purse for aspirin, she dumped two tablets into her hand and washed them down with a swallow of tap water. Her reflection flashed in the mirror as she stepped away from the sink, triggering a brief pause to study what Travis Conroy had seen.

The fluorescent tubes glared down on light hazel eyes, artfully lined and shadowed, framed by a square-jawed face and crowned by a sleek, golden cap of chin-length hair. Eden had done everything possible to change her image since high school, but somehow it wasn't enough. She had never quite broken clear of dateless, bookish Edna Rae Harper, whose romantic fantasies had colored the drabness of her life. She'd seen proof of that today when the object of those fantasies had recognized her on sight.

She leaned closer, drawn by a tiny dark mascara smudge at the corner of her left eye. Only after she'd dabbed it away with a moistened fingertip did Eden notice something else reflected in the glass—the line of urinals on the opposite wall.

For the space of a heartbeat she stood frozen, unable to believe what she'd done. Then a flush echoed from inside one of the stalls. The sound catapulted Eden into a panic. Snatching up her briefcase, she bolted out of the men's room like a spooked jackrabbit, high heels skittering on the polished tile.

Travis Conroy was standing exactly where she had left him. He didn't say a word—but then, he didn't have to. The subtly condescending quirk of one black eyebrow told her exactly what he was thinking.

She plumbed her wits for a clever comment that would put him in his place. Coming up with nothing, she shot him a look of sheer malevolence, executed an abrupt left face and stalked indignantly into the women's rest room.

Slamming into a stall, she pressed quivering hands to her hot face. Now she knew why she didn't come home more often. All she had to do was get off the plane! All she had to do was breathe the thin mountain air, and she turned into Edna Rae again—bashful, clumsy, humiliating herself at every turn!

By the time she'd finished in the stall and washed her hands, Eden had calmed down some. She had no business behaving like an adolescent, she chastised herself. She was all grown-up now. It was time she started acting that way.

Monroe, Utah, was a small town, and she planned to be there for nearly a month. As matters stood, she had a choice. She could settle things with Travis Conroy here and now, or she could repeat the same idiotic performance every time they ran into each other. It was up to her to do the intelligent thing.

Facing herself in the mirror, Eden freshened her lipstick, smoothed her hair and squared her shoulders. She would handle this like a pro, she assured herself. She would be

cool, detached and assertive. Travis Conroy was nothing but
a small-town nobody. She had absolutely no reason to feel
intimidated by him.

All the same, as she walked out of the rest room, Eden's
heart danced a skittish little tango of fear. What she was
about to do would be as difficult as anything she'd ever done
in her life.

Travis lowered his lanky frame onto a Naugahyde settee,
hooked his Stetson over one angled leg and flipped open the
paperback. The book was a fast-paced thriller by one of his
favorite authors, but today, for some reason, he couldn't
keep his mind on the plot.

Turning a page, he glanced impatiently at his watch. Nicole's flight from L.A. wouldn't be in for fifteen or twenty
minutes. If he could get through the next couple of chap-
ters . . .

Oh, what the hell!

The book dropped to his lap as he surrendered to the
angst he'd held in check since his first glimpse of the woman
who called herself Eden Harper.

It was over, Travis reminded himself. He'd had sixteen
years to put the whole silly incident behind him. By any
measure, that was time enough.

So why were his emotions churning like the agitator in an
old-fashioned Maytag?

This was crazy.

Checking his watch again, Travis shifted his buttocks
against the sagging upholstery and tried to concentrate on
his reading. But it was no good. The past was pushing into
his thoughts, crowding out his efforts to forget.

And right there on the front line was Edna Rae Harper.

Travis slumped in his seat, remembering.

It had been his senior year—the year he'd captained the
team that won its second straight Class A basketball cham-
pionship. Edna Rae had been a sophomore then, younger

than her classmates because she'd been double-promoted back in grade school.

Not that Travis had cared one way or the other. With her frumpy clothes, her horn-rimmed glasses and her way of staring at the floor when she walked down the halls, Edna Rae Harper hadn't exactly been his dream girl—or anybody else's, for that matter.

Travis had never given her a second glance. In fact, he'd scarcely been aware she existed, until that May afternoon when the year-end edition of the school paper was passed out.

Between the folds of each paper, someone had slipped a photocopied letter—a letter penned in a hand as delicate and feminine as the curl of a morning-glory vine.

Oh, Travis, my darling, when will we be together again? How long must I burn like this, tossing in my bed, feeling your hands on my pulsing breasts, feeling the velvet warmth of your skin and the sweet hot wine of your lips? How long before I hear your voice murmuring in my ear, I love you, Edna Rae, I love—

"Hello again."

Eden's breathy contralto, coming from directly behind him, jolted Travis back to the present. He swiveled in his seat to look at her, his eyes taking in the clean square planes of her face, the taffy gold mass of her hair and the chic drape of the expensive pantsuit on her slender frame. For whatever it was worth, drab little Edna Rae had grown up to be a stunner.

"Uh, hello," he replied, caught off guard. After the way she'd gone dashing off, the last thing he'd expected was to have her show up again.

She came around the back of the settee, eyes downcast, cheeks becomingly flushed. Travis watched her in silence, liking her walk, liking, in spite of everything, the catlike way she lowered herself onto the edge of the chair that faced him across the low table. The image of her, bolting crimson-faced out of the men's room, stole into his mind, coaxing his mouth into a bemused smile.

"I came to apologize," she said.

In the tick of silence that followed, Travis was aware of a jet screaming down the runway outside the window.

"Apologize? For what?" he forced himself to ask.

"For today. For this whole silly mess. I was hiding out in the rest room when I realized I was being a defensive fool, and that none of what I was feeling was your fault. I'm sorry for that."

"There's no need to be sorry about anything." He mouthed the words, wondering where all this was leading. A typical woman would not apologize unless she had some agenda in mind. But then, there'd never been anything typical about Edna Rae Harper.

She stared awkwardly at her hands, looking, at that instant, more like the shy Edna Rae than the polished Eden. "I realized something else, too. In the sixteen years since that awful day at school, I've never told you how sorry I was for the embarrassment I caused you."

"I...never expected you to." Travis forced himself to meet her eyes, wishing she'd chosen to talk about something else. His classmates had ribbed him mercilessly about that damn fool letter, but at least most of them had realized he was innocent. Not so the townspeople. By the time the story had circulated through the little community, Travis's reputation had blackened to the hue of coal tar.

"You didn't exactly have it easy yourself, did you?" he asked, shifting the burden of conversation back to her.

Eden's gaze flickered to her lap again. She hadn't come back to school for the rest of the year, Travis recalled. Her mother had claimed she was sick and received permission for the humiliated girl to complete her last two weeks of schoolwork by correspondence.

"That ridiculous letter was private," she said, staring down at her manicured hands with their pale peach nails. "I never meant anyone to see it, especially you."

"I know that," Travis feigned a detachment he did not feel. "How were you to know that Howie Segmiller would find the letter in your looseleaf and make copies for the whole school?"

A shudder passed through Eden's slim controlled body. "I... I'm sorry. I was so wrapped up in my own problems that I couldn't even think about yours. I can only imagine how much difficulty that letter must have caused you."

Travis's restless fingers curled the paperback into a thick roll. He'd been going steady with Cheryl McKinley, the prettiest girl in the junior class, he recalled. Three days after the letter incident, Cheryl had informed him that her parents wouldn't let her date him anymore.

Cheryl had married a beet farmer from Sigurd and had five kids now. He had gone off to the University of Utah and met Diane.

"It's over, Eden," he said with a shrug. "Water under the bridge, as they say. We're both different people now."

"Yes...I suppose we are." She managed a strained smile. "Whatever happened to Howie Segmiller, anyway?"

"Last time I spoke with his mother, he was running for city council in Pioche, Nevada."

"I was hoping to hear he was doing time at Point of the Mountain!" She managed a husky little laugh—fragile but real. Travis found himself wanting to hear it again.

"Howie Segmiller a jailbird?" He shook his head, chuckling. "Oh, Howie was no angel, I'll grant you. But he was too smart to get more than a hand slap. Perfect political material!"

Eden did laugh then, a surprisingly delicious sound, as sexy as the rustle of silk against a bare thigh. For a few seconds Travis allowed himself to bask in it, savoring the naughty little tickle it gave him.

What if he was to push the idea of giving her a ride home? He'd brought up the subject out of politeness the first time and had shrugged off her refusal with a sense of relief. But what harm would it do? The long bus trip south, with its endless string of ten-minute stops, was an ordeal nobody deserved. He could—

Forget it!

This was Edna Rae Harper, he reminded himself. He had spent years undoing the damage her dumb teenage fantasy had caused.

Some things were too hard won to risk.

Travis glanced at his watch again as a crowd of passengers spilled out of a gate and onto the concourse. Across from him, Eden stirred and reached for her briefcase.

"It's time I was going," she said. "My luggage will be coming in, and I can see that you're waiting for someone."

"I'm waiting for my daughter. But she's not due in for a few minutes yet." Travis realized he'd just issued an invitation for Eden to stick around. Strangely enough, he was enjoying her company more than he'd expected.

"Your daughter?" The sunlight slanted soft gold on her face as she leaned toward him. "So you've got a little girl!" she exclaimed with an animation that made Travis wince.

"That's right. But Nicole's not so little anymore. She turned fourteen last month."

"Fourteen." Eden hesitated, then slowly released her grip on the handle of her briefcase. "Where's she flying from?"

"California. She lives there with her mother and stepfather. I get her every summer." Travis's voice carried an edge. Nine years was plenty of time to get over Diane. But losing Nicole—that part had never stopped hurting.

Well, the hurt was about to ease, he reminded himself. A few minutes from now, the plane would be touching down on the tarmac, and Nicole would be back in his life. His little pal. His hiking, camping, fishing and riding partner for the rest of the summer. It would be wonderful to feel like a father again.

Travis watched the flight of a sea gull as it skimmed past the window and veered out over the runway. His restless fingers ruffled the pages of the paperback in his lap.

Soon, he thought. Soon.

And in the meantime, there was the intriguing Miss Harper.

Eden uncrossed her legs and smoothed out a crease in her linen slacks. Now would be the smart time to get up and leave, she admonished herself. Travis's daughter would be arriving any minute. Seeing her father with a strange woman could give the young girl a painfully wrong impression.

But Travis seemed in no hurry to have her go. He was leaning back in his seat, regarding her lazily. Was he resentful, amused or merely bored? Eden could read no clue in the smoky depths of his narrowed eyes.

She fiddled with her briefcase, her pulse clunking like a bent bicycle wheel as she grappled with this new set of realities.

Travis, divorced, with a fourteen-year-old daughter.

Travis, sitting across from her as if they had never been anything but friends.

Her restless gaze dropped to the big, sun-bronzed hand that lay across the open paperback, and she pondered his lack of wedding ring. It was impossible to believe Travis Conroy could be unattached for long. He'd had females chasing him since he was in kindergarten. All he had to do was take his pick.

Oh, what was she doing here, thinking inanities and blushing like a moron? She had to get out of here before she made a complete fool of herself.

"So tell me what you do in New York," he said, making a stab at conversation.

"Me?" Eden blinked her mind back into focus. "Oh . . . I've just been promoted to senior editor at Parnell Books. I've got my eye on my boss's job when he retires next year—that is, if some other publishing house doesn't lure me away first."

A smile flickered enticingly around his eyes. "So you're an editor. I always thought you had the brains to make something of yourself."

"Really?" The compliment had caught Eden off guard. Her heart sank as she felt the all-too-familiar flush of color creep up her throat to flood her cheeks. She groped for something to fill the excruciating silence.

"How long has it been since you've seen your daughter?" she asked lamely.

"Too long." He shifted his shoulders with a sigh. "I was supposed to have her over the Christmas holidays, but she came down with chicken pox. Diane promised me spring vacation to make up the time, but then Nicole had a chance to go to Hawaii with her cousins. She was so damned excited about it. What could I say?"

"So you haven't seen her since last fall?"

"Nope." Travis stretched his long legs, crossing his worn cowboy boots at the ankles. "And I'm getting pretty anxious. She's a special little lady. Gets good grades, plays the flute like an angel. And she likes camping and fishing almost as much as her old dad does. We're going to have a great time this summer, just—"

He broke off as the PA blared, announcing an arrival at gate B-16. "Hey! That's Nicole's flight! Come on, I'll introduce you!"

"I really don't think . . ." Eden began. But he was already out of earshot, charging down the concourse toward the swarm of deplaning passengers.

Eden hesitated. Then, resolving not to follow him, she stood up, slung her heavy briefcase over one shoulder and strode in the opposite direction, toward the escalator that led down to the baggage-claim area. It was time for a fast exit. An extra couple of hours on a bus were nothing compared to what she could get herself into by sticking around.

Except... She paused, torn by curiosity. After the way Travis had rhapsodized about his little girl, it might be interesting to see what she looked like. It would be an intriguing challenge, Eden mused, to try to pick Travis's daughter out of a crowd. Afterward, it would still be easy enough to slip away and catch a taxi for the Greyhound depot.

Impulsively she turned around and strolled back along the far side of the concourse to an unobtrusive spot that gave her a view of the gate. She could see Travis, pine-tall, straining forward as the passengers filed out of the jetway. Clearly he was still watching for his daughter.

Settling back against the wall, Eden began to play her game, assessing each female passenger who emerged through the gate. A young woman with a baby—no. A chic fiftyish matron in a designer suit—certainly not. A pubescent child-woman in sunglasses, skintight hip huggers and a formfitting crop top—hardly! A pretty, young—yes, of course! The studious-looking girl carrying a flute case, her chestnut curls tied back with a ribbon. No doubt about it. That was Nicole.

Eden glanced over at Travis. He was standing stock-still, looking as if he'd just been poleaxed.

"Nicole!" He rasped out the name as the young girl with the flute case passed him without a glance.

"Nicole, over here!"

A squeal of delight exploded from the nymphet in the skintight jeans.

"Daddy!" she warbled, hurling herself into Travis's arms with a force that nearly bowled him over. "Oh, Daddy! You can't imagine how much I've missed you!"

Chapter Two

"You've, uh, gotten taller." Still dazed, Travis braced his daughter at arm's length. His gaze took in the outsize sunglasses, the boyishly cropped hair, the white knit top that ended at mid-rib cage and was snug enough to show off her—

But never mind. There was no place below Nicole's tanned shoulders where Travis could comfortably rest his eyes.

"Aren't you glad to see me?" Her tentative smile was as flawless as a string of pearls. She'd gotten her braces off, he realized. And no one had even told him about it.

"'Glad' isn't the word for it, sweetheart. I'm just, uh, a little startled, that's all. You're not my little girl anymore. You're growing up. That's going to take some getting used to."

"All little girls grow up." She shifted her tote bag and linked an arm through his. "You wouldn't want me to be a kid forever, would you?"

"I don't know. It was pretty nice while it lasted." Travis adjusted his long strides to her smaller ones, wishing he had a blanket to fling around her nubile, exposed body. Very soon he would have to take her to task about that outfit—or lack of outfit. But not just yet. Not in their first precious minutes together.

"Hungry?" he asked her. "We could stop for burgers on our way out of town."

She shook her head like a saucy little bird. "I macked a sandwich on the plane. But I've got to run to the john." She handed him the claim check she'd fished out of her tote bag. "You go ahead and grab my stuff off the carousel. I'll catch up in a sec."

Brushing a kiss on his cheek, she released his arm and scampered into the crowd. A balding bearded male in a Budweiser T-shirt moved aside to let her pass. His eyes flicked over her body with an expression so lustful that it was all Travis could do to keep from hurling himself at the man and inflicting major damage. No, the issue of Nicole's costume could not wait a minute longer.

"Nicole!"

She glanced demurely back over her shoulder.

"Don't you have a sweatshirt or something in that bag? You need to put some clothes on."

She stared at him as if he'd just time-warped from the 1800s. "Oh, Daddy, don't be a nerd! It's the middle of June! It's summer, and these *are* my clothes!"

"Now, look, young lady..." Travis's words evaporated like spit on a hot sidewalk as Nicole flashed into the King's-X zone of the women's rest room. He stood there fuming as he struggled to come to terms with the past two minutes of his life.

In college he had sat through classes in adolescent psychology and read more books on the subject than he cared to remember. In the early years, when he'd taught high-school math to support the ranch, he'd seen scores of young girls pass into womanhood. He certainly understood that females in their teens could be difficult.

But nothing had prepared him for the emotional bronco ride of dealing with his own daughter.

Jamming his Stetson onto his head, he turned and strode up the concourse, headed for the escalator and the baggage-claim area. One thing was certain. Miss Nicole Conroy was overdue for an attitude adjustment. Once they got safely home, setting her straight would be the first priority on his list.

The ride south, which he'd been looking forward to all day, suddenly loomed as a three-hour battle with a headstrong teenager. Maybe it wouldn't be a bad idea, after all, to shanghai Eden Harper for the duration. At least, with Eden along, there'd be someone to serve as a buffer between—

Eden.

Travis swore under his breath as he realized the woman was nowhere in sight.

Halting in midstride, he turned around and scanned the length of the concourse. No Eden.

Maybe she'd already carried out her plan to take a cab to the bus station. Fine and dandy, Travis groused, growing more irritated by the minute. What had he expected? That she'd be waiting for him to grab her by the hair and drag her to the truck?

Loping back to the escalator, he caught a step for the downward ride. Below him, the baggage-claim enclosure bustled with activity as suitcases, duffels and boxes spun off the conveyors. Travis fumbled for Nicole's claim check. Glancing out over the carousels, he suddenly caught sight of Eden's sugar-blond head. She was at the far end of the floor, fidgeting impatiently with her briefcase as she waited for her bags. Probably anxious to make her getaway. Well, fine. He certainly had no right to stop her.

As the escalator glided downward, he conjured up an image of Eden waiting in the dingy bus station, then sitting up in a cramped seat next to some snoring matriarch while the bus made stops at Ephriam, at Manti, at Axtell, at Gunnison, at Centerfield . . . What the hell, it was her choice. Let her go.

As he stepped off the escalator, a glance in Eden's direction told him she had spotted her luggage. She was moving toward the carousel, shifting her briefcase to her shoulder to free her hands. *Don't borrow more trouble,* Travis's brain cautioned. But his legs weren't listening. Unbidden, they were moving fast, covering the floor in long loping strides that carried him to her side.

"Here!" he exclaimed, reaching in front of her for one of the matching charcoal gray suitcases. "At least let me haul these to the curb for you."

Dismay flickered in Eden's eyes, and Travis instantly wished he'd kept his distance. "Look," he said, "I'm not planning to talk you out of taking the bus. In fact, it's probably just as well that you *don't* ride home with me."

"I just don't want to cause any more trouble—for either of us." Her voice was frayed, like tightly strained silk. Its raw sexiness was a burr that irritated Travis to the snapping point.

"Fine, then. At least we understand—"

The words ended in a croak as he glanced up and saw Nicole coming down the escalator. She had taken off her sunglasses, and as she glided downward, her dark eyes twinkled impishly up at a blond, husky young man in a Utah State University T-shirt who shared the same step.

Travis battled the urge to grind his teeth. Nicole was saying something now, and the young hulk was grinning down at her—no, drooling was more like it. And he was no puppy, either. He looked to be at least nineteen, too damned old to be flirting with a fourteen-year-old child.

"Travis, are you all right?" Eden's voice pricked the edge of his awareness. He turned on her in sudden desperation.

"Ride with us," he rasped. "I'm not inviting you, Eden, I'm begging you. Otherwise, before we get home, I'm liable to strangle the little twit."

"Daddy!" Nicole had spun off the bottom of the escalator, and, with a breezy wave to the hulk, came bouncing toward them with the verve of a half-grown shelty. Watching her, Travis groaned inwardly. How could a father broach the subject of wearing a decent bra to his daughter?

"Hey, you're waiting in the wrong place," she said. "My bags'll be coming off on number three..." Her voice trailed off as her gaze flickered to Eden's sleek gray Pullman dangling from Travis's hand, and then to Eden herself, who was scrambling to retrieve the matching garment bag.

"Uh...hi." Nicole's voice quavered uncertainly.

Sensing her mistaken impression, Travis stepped in quickly. "Nicole, this is Miss Eden Harper, one of my former schoolmates. She just flew in from New York and we, uh, sort of bumped into each other on the concourse."

"Oh." Nicole's sharp brown eyes inspected Eden up and down before her face relaxed into a flippant grin. "New York, huh? That's cool."

"I'm pleased to meet you, Nicole." Eden extended a slightly nervous hand, which Nicole accepted with the jerky politeness of a marionette.

"Eden's on her way to Monroe. I've offered her a ride, and I do believe she's accepted." Travis avoided Eden's eyes. So what if he was railroading her? He was a desperate man.

"Cool." Nicole was still sizing up Eden, weighing the possibilities. "Hey, that jacket kicks!" she said. "Did you buy it in New York?"

"Uh-huh. At Bloomingdale's. On clearance, I'm afraid, but definitely Bloomingdale's." An intriguing spark danced in Eden's light green eyes. "You know, with your coloring,

I'll bet this jacket would look great on you. Why don't we find out?''

Nicole might have protested, but Eden was already shrugging out of the beige linen suit jacket. Travis blinked as Nicole dropped her tote bag and turned a submissive back, arms sliding into the proffered sleeves. Within seconds, she was modestly covered.

"What do you think?" She struck a model's pose for Eden's approval.

"Sensational!" Eden grinned. "Want to wear it home?"

"Hey, could I really?" Nicole angled her body this way and that, inspecting the lapels and pockets. "Bloomingdale's, huh? Cool."

"Come on, let's cut the fashion show and round up the baggage," Travis growled, shooting Eden a glance of unabashed gratitude. He'd half expected the woman to bolt or protest on the spot. Instead, she had smoothed things over with a deftness that left him stunned.

Avoiding his gaze, Eden turned swiftly away—but not before he'd caught a jarring glimpse of what the jacket had concealed. Eden's sleeveless peach silk blouse skimmed a curvaceous chest that he'd certainly never noticed on Edna Rae Harper. Maybe it was those baggy sweaters she'd always worn to school. Travis cursed silently as he tore his eyes away from the shadowed outline of lace beneath the gossamer-thin fabric. It was a good thing Nicole would be along to sit between them in the pickup. Otherwise, he could be in serious trouble.

Nicole's twin duffels were leaden. Travis slung one from each shoulder and, with Nicole and Eden managing the rest of the luggage, they trudged out of the elevator onto the third level of the parking terrace.

"There's the truck!" Nicole bounded ahead, dragging Eden's wheeled Pullman case behind her. Travis deliberately slowed his steps, hoping Eden would stay back with him.

"I wanted to thank you while I have the chance," he muttered, leaning close to her ear. "I was geared up for a battle royal over that outfit of hers."

The subtle aura of Eden's perfume tickled his senses as she walked deliberately ahead without glancing up at him. "Stay geared," she hissed. "This is only the first skirmish. And the rest of the war is your problem, not mine."

"You're annoyed, aren't you?"

She shot him an exasperated glance. "I just don't want any gossip when we get home. And neither do you. People in small towns have long memories."

"Well, I could always dump you in Richfield and let you hitch the last ten miles."

Eden muttered something under her breath before releasing an explosive sigh. "All right. Truce. But after this, you're on your own. I've spent sixteen years putting that awful day behind me, and nothing's going to bring it back!"

She lengthened her step, heels clicking on the concrete as her long legs carried her away from him toward the pickup where Nicole waited.

Travis hung back, his emotions churning even as his gaze followed her sensual lioness walk.

What the hell, maybe she was right. Stirring up that ridiculous old scandal would do nothing for his image in the town, especially when word got out that he and Eden had been seen together. Leave the lady alone—that would be the smart thing to do.

Smart, yes.

But as Travis inhaled, the lingering scent of her perfume aroused a warm tingle that had nothing to do with wisdom.

Eden had reached the truck. She stood waiting for him to bring the key, gazing out over the rows of parked vehicles.

Travis pulled himself together with a mental slap. What was *she* being so uppity about, anyway? *He* had been the innocent party. And *he* would be the one to take the heat if things got stirred up again. Weeks from now, Miss Eden

Harper would return to her New York world—a world so remote it might as well be on the moon. But he was the one who lived in Monroe. If anything happened between them, *he* was the one who'd be mopping up the mess.

Play it safe, Travis cautioned himself. *Leave the lady on her doorstep and forget her.*

But even as he strode toward the truck, he knew his willpower was going to have an uphill battle.

"I want to sit by the window!" Nicole hung on to the open door of the weather-beaten Ford pickup, swinging back and forth until the hinges squawked.

"Just climb in, young lady!" Travis's shoulders rippled as he hefted the baggage, including Eden's precious briefcase, into the truck's open back. The truck bed had been swept, but green hay dust clung deep in the metal grooves, rich with the smell of home.

Eden's memory stirred, recalling the small ranch Travis's family had owned west of town on Poverty Flat. She remembered warm summer evenings, riding her bike along the back roads, filling her senses with the aroma of fresh-cut hay as she pedaled slowly past his gate. She remembered the wind in her hair, the mosquito bites on her legs, the exquisite surges of longing as she gazed toward his house....

"Please, Eden!" Nicole wheedled. "I want to see out! I get claustrophobia when I sit in the middle!"

"Now, listen..." Travis turned sharply, his voice harsh with annoyance. Sensing a confrontation, Eden impulsively stepped between them.

"It's all right," she said swiftly. "I really don't mind sitting in the middle of the seat. Let Nicole have the window, if that's what she wants."

The thunderous scowl Travis flashed her made Eden realize she had overstepped her bounds, but he said nothing to confirm it. With a curt "Suit yourself," he swung away, leaving her to scramble gracelessly into the high cab on her own while he secured the tailgate. She slid across the blanket-upholstered seat and straddled the gearbox with her legs, bracing for a very long three-hour ride.

Nicole plopped in beside her, grinning as she slammed the door of the truck and began rolling down the window. "Thanks. You're cool, Eden. And I can already tell my daddy's got the hots for you."

"Nicole!" Eden's heart sank as she felt the detested blush flame her cheeks. "You don't know what you're—"

"Psych!"

Nicole giggled, then, seeing Eden's puzzled expression, she explained, "That means I was just kidding—wanted to see what you'd do. Boy, I'm sure glad I don't blush like that! Hey, look at that buff guy..." She swiveled toward the open window, craning her neck to see past the side mirror.

Eden shrank into the upholstery, willing herself to vanish as Travis swung in beside her and buckled himself into the driver's seat. Too late, she realized what close quarters the inside of a pickup truck could be. Barring visible contortions, there was no way she could sit comfortably without pressing against him from shoulder to knee.

A flutter of panic teased Eden's diaphragm, climaxing in a nervous hiccup. Travis's eyes stared straight ahead beneath the brim of his Stetson, as if she did not exist. His jaw tightened as he jammed the key into the ignition, then, as the engine roared to life, thrust his hand between her knees to grab the gearshift knob. Eden pressed her lips together as the oddly intimate contact touched off a little scherzo of hiccups.

Edna Rae had returned in all her glory.

Travis shot her a sidelong glance as he backed out of the parking space. "Put your seat belts on, ladies," was all he said.

"Oh, you're such an old fussbudget!" Nicole fumed. But she did snap her shoulder harness, then reach around to help drag the ends of Eden's lap belt from under the back of the seat.

"Daddy, we need to stop and get sodas," she piped up.

Travis ignored her. His elbow grazed Eden's breast as he negotiated the corkscrew exit of the airport parking garage, igniting a tingle of awareness that caused them both to jerk apart.

"We need sodas," Nicole persisted. "Eden's got the hiccups. Listen."

"I'm fine—really." Eden punctuated her protest with an ill-timed *hic* as Travis pulled through the parking tollgate.

"Well, the sodas are going to have to wait till we get a few miles down the freeway," he said. "There's no place to stop out here."

"Please don't bother on my account," Eden said, feeling woefully out of place. She did not belong in this role, playing buffer between a father and his willful young daughter. She especially did not belong in this truck, scrunched tight against the man who had made her pulse skitter since she was as young as Nicole. She was sick and tired of attractive males. Most of them, she'd sadly learned, were bullying, self-centered manipulators, and Travis Conroy was clearly no exception.

So why, then, was she reacting to him like a teenager in hormone overdrive?

Eden sat rigid as glass, excruciatingly aware of the heat that simmered along the line where her thigh lay against his. He smelled of the outdoors, of grass and sun and the kind of good, plain supermarket soap her mother always bought on sale. His flesh was warm and hard through the worn fabric of his jeans.

She took a deep breath, struggling to ignore the forbidden flutters his touch aroused in her body. A downward glance confirmed that her nipples had shrunk to tight little raspberries. They stood out through the wispy silk of a blouse she would never have chosen to wear without the concealing jacket. Too late, she missed the briefcase she'd allowed Travis to stow in the back. At least, she could have clutched it to her chest and hidden herself behind it.

Eden hiccuped wretchedly as the dry summer wind blasted her face through Nicole's open window. The bus would have had air-conditioning, but she had no right to complain. She'd gotten herself into this mess. If she was miserable, it was no more than she deserved.

Lending Nicole her jacket had been an act of pure impulse, well motivated perhaps, but not well thought out. She had wanted to be friendly to the girl and to ease Travis's obvious discomfort with her appearance. It had not occurred to her that she was walking into her own trap until it was too late to back out.

But why had she really done it? Eden scrunched into the Navajo-blanket upholstery, lost in speculation. Did she feel some need to repay Travis Conroy for the embarrassment she'd caused? Or had she just wanted to show him that she was a big girl now, and savvy enough to handle a willful fourteen-year-old?

Oh, what was she doing here? If she had any sense, she would leap out of the truck, flag down a taxi and head straight for the bus depot!

The worst part was the way Travis had lapped it all up. He probably thought she was great with teenage girls. Well, she wasn't. Apart from the memories of her own painful adolescence, she understood nothing about them, especially pretty, self-assured creatures like Nicole. To her, they were like bubbly little space aliens, beings from a world she had always envied but never inhabited.

Travis's knuckles bumped her knees as the truck growled into second gear. Eden tensed, fearful of what the contact might arouse in her.

She could hold her own in the workplace, where she knew exactly what was expected. But when it came to relationships, especially with men, Edna Rae was alive and well. A

few months ago she had almost believed she could change—
but no, she could not afford to think about her broken engagement now. She would only get maudlin, and that
wouldn't do. Especially not in front of Travis Conroy.

She would make the best of the next three hours, Eden
resolved with a hiccuping sigh. She would be civil to Travis
and patient with the high-spirited Nicole. And when the ride
was over, she would thank them kindly and run for her
life—or at least for her sanity.

She would have to.

Any way you looked at him, Travis Conroy was trouble,
more trouble than she ever wanted to deal with again.

Travis shifted into third, his wrist skimming Eden's thigh
as the truck ground up the on-ramp and nosed onto the interstate. He was making every effort to appear cool, but the
veneer was already wearing thin. The changes in Nicole had
thrown him off balance, and now, with no time to recover,
he found himself plastered side by side against one of the
most disturbingly attractive females he had ever encountered.

And the hell of it was, she was Edna Rae Harper.

This was crazy, Travis lashed himself as he gunned the
engine and roared into the center lane. This lady was the
original ugly duckling. Worse, her misguided fantasies had
triggered one of the most embarrassing episodes of his life.

All he had ever wanted to do with Edna Rae Harper was
forget her.

He stared fixedly at the black butt of the Pontiac Le-
Mans in front of him, doing his damnedest to keep his eyes
off Eden's peach silk blouse. The way the fabric clung— No,
he vowed, not one glance. But even the best intent could not
stop his imagination from working. Her fragrant warmth
invaded his senses, stirring a vision of ripe peaches in the
summer sun, round, lush, silky to the touch of his fingertips...

It was enough to make a man sweat.

"So, uh, how long do you plan to be in Monroe?" he asked, making a lame stab at conversation.

Eden's bare arm grazed his shoulder as she shifted in her seat. "Let's see…I'll be running my mother back to Provo tomorrow, and they'll be doing her hysterectomy the next morning at Utah Valley Regional. After that, maybe four or five weeks, depending on how fast she recovers."

"At least you'll have a vacation from your job."

"Not really. That heavy briefcase you put in the back is full of manuscripts to read and edit."

"Hey, you're an editor?" Nicole, who'd been hanging out the window like a happy Labrador retriever, popped her head back into the cab. "That's cool. Do you work with any kickin' writers, like Stephen King?"

"I'm afraid not. Parnell is an educational textbook company. Compared to Stephen King, most of the stuff I work on is pretty dry."

"Textbooks! Yuck!" Nicole twisted back toward the open window to wave at the blond male driver of a red Corvette. Travis ground his teeth, biting back the temptation to lecture her. Nicole was just keyed up from the trip, that was all. She would settle down fine after a day or two on the ranch. Then everything would be just like old times.

Eden was gazing past him now, toward the rugged Wasatch Mountains that jutted between the city and the eastern sky. "I noticed traces of hay in the back of the truck," she ventured. "Does that mean you're working the old family ranch?"

Travis forced a sidelong grin. "You *have* been away a long time," he said. "I moved back to the ranch when I finished college. Been there ever since."

"Ranching." Eden fidgeted with her nails. "Somehow I always imagined you in a more glamorous role, like a sportscaster, or an FBI agent, or a male super model."

"Oh, nothing of the sort. Running that ranch is all I ever wanted to do." Travis edged the truck around the small Pontiac, striving to ignore the womanly warmth of Eden's leg and the sensually whispered message of her perfume. *Edna Rae Harper.* He rolled the name in his mind as he took a deep breath and continued speaking.

"My dad barely made enough on the place to keep the family fed. The land's too dry and rocky for most crops. Even the few cows he kept were poor milkers. But ten years ago, I started raising quarter horses. The horses do fine with extra hay and oats, and since I mortgaged the place to pick up a champion stud, the colts have been bringing decent money in Vegas and L.A."

"You sound like a satisfied man." She settled back into the seat beside him, the hot wind bannering her spun-honey hair.

"Satisfied?" Travis let the question hang on the air. If "satisfied" meant coming home to an empty house and eating supper alone, then drifting into solitary slumber in the big brass bed where his parents had conceived five children...

"Uh-huh," he nodded, feigning smugness, "you might say I've done all right by the old place."

"It sounds as if you have no plans to leave." Eden stirred, her breast brushing his sleeve with the impact of a rocket burst.

"Leave?" Travis's attempted chuckle came out sounding hollow. "My grandpa bought that land west of town when he came home from the First World War. My dad spent his whole life there, battling rocks and tumbleweeds to grub out a livelihood. He and Mom raised five kids before they passed on. I was the baby of the family—but then, I guess you know all that.

"Over the years, as I watched my brothers and sisters spread their wings, I promised myself that after I got my

education, I'd come back and take care of the ranch, maybe
even make something fine of it one day."

He paused for breath. He'd been talking too much, he
realized. Probably making a bore of himself. What was
wrong with him today, anyway? With the women he occa-
sionally dated, he was never at a loss for clever flattering
things to say. But in the thirty-odd minutes he'd spent with
Eden Harper, he'd done little more than talk about himself. He'd already unloaded a good chunk of his life in her
lap. If he didn't stop soon—

"Hey!" he announced, seizing the moment. "I see a
Circle K sign just past that off-ramp. Anybody for sodas?"

"Me!" Nicole jerked her head back inside the cab. "I'll
have an extra-large Diet Coke. And can I have some Chee-
tos, too? And a Milky Way?"

"Sure." Travis pulled into the exit lane, grateful that at
least one thing about Nicole—her appetite—hadn't
changed. "What's your pleasure, Eden?"

"Uh . . . iced tea. Plain. And thank you."

"You won't get much nourishment out of that. Sure
can't get you a hot dog or something?"

"I had lunch on the plane. Tea will be fine."

"Hey, Eden!" Nicole grinned. "I think your hiccups are
gone!"

"Oh . . ." Eden blinked, then, as if on cue, emitted a lusty
hic. Her cheeks flushed appealingly as she shrugged, then
laughed, shaking her wind-tangled hair. She looked damned
sexy, Travis observed. And he knew some very interesting
cures for the hiccups. The thought flashed through his mind
that, under different circumstances, he wouldn't mind trying some of them on her.

But this was crazy, he reminded himself with a sharp
mental slap. People in small towns had memories like elephants. Take up with Edna Rae Harper, and the whole idiotic scandal would come crashing down on their heads
again.

Forcing his mind back to the present, he swung the truck into the parking lot. "Hold down the fort, ladies. I'll be right back," he said, swinging out of the cab. "Let's see—extra-large Diet Coke, Chee-tos, a Milky Way and one plain iced tea. Right?"

"Right," said Nicole. "And a pack of Big Red."

"Got it." Travis clicked shut the door of the truck and strode into the convenience store. He hadn't decided what to get for himself, except that it would need to be large, wet and cold.

Damned cold.

"Did you really go to school with my dad? Wow, it must have been a long time ago!"

Thanks a lot, kid! Eden squirmed under Nicole's open scrutiny, feeling like a frog on a dissecting table. Travis had been gone about twenty seconds, and she was already getting the third degree.

"Longer than your whole lifetime," she answered pleasantly. "Your father graduated two years before I did."

"And did you think my dad was hot?"

"Nicole . . ." Eden's cheeks blazed like neon.

"A lot of girls do, you know. Even now that he's so old. And the women in town—God, you should see them!"

"Don't swear, Nicole. Your father wouldn't like it."

"But you wouldn't believe them! Calling him on the phone! Bringing him pies and brownies and chicken casseroles! Inviting him over for supper, and who knows what else! He could marry any one of them in a minute. But he won't. Want to know why?"

"That really isn't any of my business," Eden forced herself to say.

Nicole ran a hand through her gamine thatch of dark brown curls. "Want to know?"

"Nicole—" Eden's protest ended in another hiccup. "All right. Why?"

"Because he's still in love with my mom, that's why. After all these years, he's never gotten over her. That's why he hasn't found anybody else." Nicole studied her pert reflection in the side mirror. "So, you didn't answer my question. When you were in high school, did you think my dad was hot?"

Eden exhaled in defeat. "All the girls thought so. I guess I did, too."

Nicole leaned closer to the mirror, squinting at an imaginary blemish. "Know what a girl in his high school did? She wrote this mash letter to my dad in her notebook. Real X-rated stuff, from what I heard. Some boy found the letter and passed out copies with the school paper. Poor Daddy was embarrassed to death, and I guess it just about ruined his reputation for good."

Eden had gone cold in the stifling heat of the cab. "Where," she managed to ask, "did you ever hear such a story?"

"From Kim Driscoll. Last summer. Kim said the girl's name was Agnes or something, and that she was a real nerd. She left town after graduation and never came back. Did you know her, Eden?"

Eden shook her head in feeble denial, casting urgent glances past the gas pumps to the entrance of the Circle K where Travis had just stepped outside.

"Run and help your father, Nicole," she said. "He looks as if he might be about to drop those big drinks."

"Right!" Travis's daughter flashed out of the truck to bound across the asphalt in the swimming heat. Eden sagged limply against the upholstery, her silk blouse clinging to her skin. Her stomach clenched as she faced the reality of going home to the place where people still talked about Edna Rae Harper.

How could she do it? After what her ridiculous teenage fantasizing had done to Travis, how could she show her face in town again?

Worse, how could she avoid it?

On her other rare visits to Monroe, she had simply stayed out of sight. This time, Eden realized, hiding would not be an option. There would be shopping to do, errands to run, callers to greet. For the period of her mother's recovery, she would have no choice except to deal with people who hadn't seen her in years, but who still remembered the scandal and, evidently, still talked about it.

She would rise to the challenge, Eden resolved grimly. She would smile and hold her head high, as if the disgrace had never happened. Her conduct would be above reproach; and that would include keeping a wide country mile between herself and Travis Conroy.

That part, Eden assured herself, would be easy. After this miserable trip, Travis would never want to see her again, and the sentiment was mutual. The cookie-and-casserole crowd could have him—that is, if any of them could lure him away from the memory of his ex-wife.

"Your tea, milady."

Eden's eyes fluttered open as something cold and wet slid along her cheek. She had dozed off, she suddenly realized. And Travis was beside her, touching her hot face with the chilled, glistening bottle of iced tea.

"Feel good?" He met her startled gaze with a grin as the glassy coolness slipped dreamily down the curve of her throat, to pause at the neckline of her damp silk blouse. Eden's eyelids floated shut, then jerked open again.

"Give me that!" Flustered and confused, she snatched the bottle out of his hand. "Wh-where's Nicole?"

"Inside, buying the toothbrush she forgot to pack." He swung into the seat beside her, balancing a bucket-size cold-drink cup in his left hand. "Sorry it's so hot in here. My next truck will have air-conditioning, I promise."

"If my memory doesn't fail me, there's a Ford dealer-ship off the next exit."

"Very funny." He tossed Nicole's snacks onto her seat then leaned back and took a long pull on his straw. "You'r all right, Eden Harper. You've got class."

Eden forced her hazy mind to generate a response. "Mor class than Edna Rae?"

A shadow flickered across his face, then swiftly van ished. "Edna Rae had class, too," he said. "She just didn' know it." Without asking, he reclaimed her iced-tea bottl and twisted off the lid. "Here, drink up. It'll help cool yo off."

Accepting the tea, Eden tilted back her head and let it lovely brisk coldness trickle down her throat. She'd gotte up at 4:30 a.m. to catch a cab to La Guardia for the fligh west. She was sweaty and exhausted. Her clothes were glue to her body, her hair was a windblown mess, and the aspi rin she'd taken earlier hadn't even made a dent in her head ache.

But at least, she realized, her hiccups had stopped.

She cradled the icy bottle between her palms, painfull conscious of Travis's presence beside her. Striving for an ai of cool detachment, she raised the bottle to her lips and too a deep swallow. The tea went down her windpipe. She coughed and sputtered, wishing passionately that she coul just melt into the floorboard and disappear.

"Hey, are you okay?" The edge in Travis's voice coul have been either concern or amusement.

She nodded, struggling against the cough reflex. "I'm... fine. It's just . . . Edna Rae, coming back to . . . haunt me."

Again, that odd dark shadow flickered across his face "Eden, you don't have to—"

He broke off as Nicole came bounding into sight, waving the toothbrush she'd bought. Eden felt a prickle of relief Forget the past, she told herself. Forget it all. That was the only sensible thing to do.

Nicole popped into the cab and slammed the door hard. Her free hand darted to the radio, flipped on the power switch and punched the select buttons till the heavy-metal beat of a local rock station blared out of the speakers.

"Okay, Daddy?" she shouted over the volume.

"Eden?" Travis shot her a questioning glance.

"Fine." Eden slumped into the seat cushions, her head throbbing in rhythm with the beat. She'd long since outgrown her taste for hard rock, but at least with the music blasting, she wouldn't be expected to carry on a conversation.

"Seat belts, ladies!" Travis swung the truck out of the parking lot and back toward the freeway. Eden complied groggily as the long day's fatigue caught up with her. The traffic, the billboards and the gray-green June landscape swam and blurred in her vision. Even Nicole's radio music dimmed as her eyelids grew heavier...

Travis exhaled as the weight of Eden's head plopped against his shoulder. *Take it easy,* he cautioned himself as he worked his hand between her linen-clad knees to reach the gearshift knob. *Just shift your mind into neutral and keep it there until you've left this lady where she belongs.*

Moving slowly, he put the truck into high gear and cranked the growling engine up to sixty-five for the long drive home. His eyes risked a glance at her sleeping face, even as he battled the temptation to let his gaze drift lower.

No, he reflected darkly, it had not been a smart idea, bringing her along. Over the years, he had managed to distance himself from Edna Rae and the trouble she'd caused him. He had buried her image, freezing it in the past like a photograph in an old high-school yearbook. For a long time now, he had felt safe.

But he could feel safe no longer. Not with Eden's sleepy weight against his arm. Not with her hair blowing soft and pale against his sleeve and the warm damp sensuality of her fragrance curling in his nostrils.

Edna Rae was back, invading his life with an impact he had never imagined. It was as if some long-barred door inside him had cracked open, and he could not see what was on the other side. He was intrigued, Travis conceded. He was also confused, angry, and plain damned scared.

The only sensible course was to play it cool. Be friendly with the lady. Talk to her. Joke with her as if nothing had happened. Then leave her at her front door and run like a five-point buck.

He had put the past behind him. Nothing—not even a sexy, vulnerable, funny lady with spun-sugar hair—was worth bringing it back.

Chapter Three

The sun cast long fingers of shadow over the scrub-dotted hills as Travis pulled off the freeway at the Scipio cutoff. Nicole's rock station had faded into static. Nicole had faded with it. She was curled sound asleep against the locked door, the half-empty bag of Chee-tos still clutched in her lap.

He reached out and switched off the radio, welcoming the silence. Eden stirred against his shoulder, whimpered like a dreaming pup and settled back into slumber. Her perfume had mellowed, blending with her own musky scent in a mélange that Travis found disturbingly erotic. For a man who savored smell, touch and taste, as well as sight, he reflected, Eden Harper possessed the makings of a sensual banquet.

The day had been long and hot. Travis was tired—too tired to stop his mind from imagining how that banquet would progress. He would start by nuzzling the windblown honey of her hair, then move on to explore the salty involuted shell of her ear with his tongue tip, taking time to nibble his way around to her mango-sweet lips and savor the dark wine-moist secrets of her mouth. Next he would ease up the hem of that luscious peach blouse and ripple his hands slowly over her—

Damn!

What the devil did he think he was doing? This was Edna Rae Harper he was getting so worked up about! Edna Rae, whose unrequited crush had touched off the biggest disaster of his high-school years.

But not, by any means, the biggest disaster of his life.

He had not wanted the divorce. But looking back from a perspective of nine years, he could see that the split with Diane had been inevitable. They had married far too young and become parents before either of them was ready. For Diane, raised in the posh world of Newport Beach, life in a tiny two-room apartment, with no money, a demanding baby and a husband preoccupied with school and work, must have been hell on earth.

A coyote darted out of the junipers and flashed across the road, a gray phantom in the twilight. Travis switched on the headlights and swung his attention back to his driving. There were plenty of deer on this road, not to mention stray cattle. It wouldn't do to hit something or to swerve off the shoulder of the two-lane highway and roll into the barrow pit. Not with such precious cargo aboard.

His tired eyes gazed ahead of the lights, at the long blue ribbon of road. Things might have worked out differently if he'd done things Diane's way, he reflected. But when he'd insisted on returning to Monroe and had taken a job at the high school . . . yes, it was a wonder the marriage had lasted as long as it did. Diane had hated small-town life. She had hated the ranch. Only Nicole had held them together. And in the end, even Nicole hadn't been enough.

He glanced tenderly over at his daughter where she sprawled in her seat, wrapped in Eden's jacket, clutching her Chee-tos as she slept. He hadn't lost her, he reminded himself. She was here. She was his for the whole summer.

And things were bound to be all right between them. For all her grown-up airs, she was still his little girl. She was only fourteen, and she needed her father as much as she had ever needed him in her tender young life.

He would make the most of this summer, Travis promised himself. He would plan his time around being with Nicole, sharing fun, forging bonds of love and trust to last through the long months of separation.

As for Eden Harper, she had given him a turn, but the lady was only passing through. In an hour's time, he would be unloading her bags in her driveway. If he had any sense, he would bid her a breezy farewell and put her out of his mind for good.

If he had any sense.

Aye, as Hamlet would say, there was the rub.

Eden's head moved against his shoulder, her silky hair skimming his throat like a breath. The unexpected warmth that trickled through Travis's body was so sweet that he almost moaned out loud.

No, he conceded, it wasn't going to be that simple. Drab little Edna Rae Harper had evolved into a delicious woman, as tempting as homemade peach-vanilla ice cream on a hot summer day. The urge to steal a taste would torment him for as long as she was in town. If he allowed himself to weaken . . .

But he couldn't afford to think of Eden now. Not while he was warm and muzzy and surrounded by the fragrant cocoon of her nearness. Any decision involving Miss Eden Harper would have to be made at a safe distance, with a cool clear head.

Travis dimmed his running lights as a car swished past in the opposite direction, headed for Scipio and the freeway. The sky was streaked with crimson above the escarpment that rimmed the lonesome little valley. The evening breeze was cool through the open window.

Restless now, he felt Eden's sleepy weight against his arm and thought of home.

"Rise and shine, city lady."

"Mmm?" Eden opened her eyes to Travis's sinfully dimpled smile. His face was a hand's breath from her own, so close that it startled her. She jerked backward.

He chuckled under his breath. "Wake up, Miss Harper. You're home."

"Oh..." She struggled upright as the truck's dim interior swam into focus, including Nicole, sound asleep on her right.

"For what it's worth, I came into town by the back road," Travis whispered. "Nobody saw us. Our reputations remain unsullied."

"Oh, shush!" Eden was too groggy and uncomfortable for pleasantries. The jab she gave his ribs was only half in jest. "Just get out of my way, and I'll see if I can slide under the steering wheel and make my exit without disturbing your daughter."

"Right." With the engine still idling, he eased open the door of the pickup and dropped lightly to the ground. Eden forced her sleep-numbed body to stir. Sweat had plastered her clothes to her skin. The fabric shifted itchily as she slid across the seat. She did not even want to imagine what her face and hair must look like.

The driver's seat was warmly indented with the imprint of Travis's lean buttocks. He stood watching, eyes glinting sardonically as she slid beneath the steering wheel. Outside, it was almost fully dark—about nine-thirty, Eden calculated. She was grateful for the lateness of the hour and the quietness of the street. No one, not even her mother, seemed to have heard the truck pull into the driveway.

"Careful, it's a long drop to the ground." His hands reached up to help her out the door. In her groggy disheveled state, Eden wanted no part of him.

"It's all right, I can make it by myself!" she snapped. And she might have done just that, except for the fact that her leg had gone to sleep somewhere past Yuba Lake. The benumbed foot that groped for a toehold missed the edge entirely. Eden tumbled backward into Travis's waiting arms.

He caught her deftly by the waist, his strong hands supporting her from behind as he lowered her to the ground. "Easy now." His voice, husky with amusement, droned in her ear like a big fuzzy bumblebee. "You'd better watch your step, Miss Harper. What will the neighbors think?"

For Eden, it was the last straw.

"Oh, leave me alone!" she muttered, twisting loose and turning to glower up at him. "All right, I admit it. From the first second I saw you at the airport, I've done nothing but make a fool of myself. But you don't have to rub it in. The least you can do is leave me with some...dignity!"

Her voice cracked on the last word as she struggled for self-control. She might have wheeled and stormed into the house, but her luggage, she realized, was still in the back of the pickup.

"You've been laughing at me all afternoon!" she fumed. "Klutzy little Edna Rae, always stumbling over her own feet! Well, I'm not Edna Rae anymore! In fact, Edna Rae doesn't even—"

"May I tell you something?" Travis's grin had faded, but a hint of cockiness still flickered in the depths of his mahogany eyes.

"Get my suitcases down, please," Eden retorted icily. "After that I'll listen to whatever you have to say."

"Anything to please a lady!" He swung toward the back of the truck, caught up Eden's bags and briefcase, and piled them in the driveway. That done, he stood facing her, his broad-shouldered presence blocking out the almond moon where it floated above the jagged mountain skyline.

"And now will you hear me out?"

"As long as it's not a lecture." Eden braced her emotional barricades against his charm. One thing hadn't changed since high school, she realized with a sinking heart. Travis Conroy still had the power to reduce her to a quivering lump of jelly.

But this time she would not let him do it. She wasn't a palpitating teenager anymore. She was a grown woman with an independent life. And Travis was no longer her idol. He was a man, nothing more.

"I'm ready," she said. "So, what was it you wanted to tell me?"

"Just this." He caught her hand, trapping it like a bird in the curl of his hard-callused palm. "I know I sort of railroaded you into coming along, but I truly can't say that I'm sorry. Thanks for being such a good sport. You're a breath of fresh air, Eden Harper."

Thrown off balance by his evident sincerity, Eden groped for a fitting reply. But before she could speak, he raised her hand to his lips and skimmed a courtly kiss across her knuckles.

"Good night, sweet princess," he murmured, his eyes twinkling with rapier-edged humor, "and farewell."

"Oh..." Eden sputtered, stung by the subtle mockery of his gesture. "Oh, you..."

But Travis could not hear her, she realized. He had vaulted into the seat of the pickup, and the big vehicle was already rolling out of the drive. She stood dry-mouthed, her hand still tingling from the brush of his lips as the truck pulled into the street and roared away.

The red taillights had vanished around the corner by the time Eden recovered her wits. *Good riddance,* she fumed as the well-remembered stomach flutters subsided. Travis Conroy was the most exasperating person she had ever known. That she had once been so naive as to worship him... No, it was beyond belief!

But enough of Travis. She had come a long way, and she was exhausted. Right now all she wanted to do was hug her mother, trudge upstairs to a long relaxing shower and slide between a set of lovely cool cotton sheets.

Eden hefted the Pullman onto the porch of the neat stucco house and went back for the other bags. The place seemed unusually quiet. Madge Harper's familiar green '89 Buick was parked in the carport, but no light was visible through the drawn living-room curtains.

Her mother would be expecting her arrival on the late-night bus, Eden reminded herself. She had probably gone to bed early to get some sleep before meeting her daughter at the drugstore where the bus dropped its passengers. There was no need to disturb her, Eden decided. Not if she could manage to sneak inside without being heard.

She tried the door. It was locked, but no matter. The spare house key would be under the round rock in the geranium bed where her mother had kept it for years. A moment's rummaging, and Eden had it in her hand.

Brushing damp earth from the tarnished brass, she scooted her bags up to the threshold and thrust the key into the lock. The tumblers dropped soundlessly, freeing the door to swing open on well-oiled hinges.

Hefting her briefcase and garment bag, Eden stumbled into the darkened entryway. A little light wouldn't hurt, she mused, leaning to nudge the familiar switch with her left shoulder.

"Oh!"

Her bags thudded to the floor as the couple entwined in a passionate embrace on the living-room sofa gasped and broke apart.

"Mom!" Eden blinked in shocked disbelief.

"Uh, hello, dear." Madge Harper, pink-faced and curiously radiant, stumbled to her feet, rippling a nervous hand through her short gray hair. "What a surprise! I wasn't expecting you for hours yet!"

"I . . . know." Eden's eyes darted to the middle-aged man on the sofa, who was struggling to rearrange his Lincolnesque features into some semblance of dignity. His face was not unfamiliar, but in her flustered state, Eden could not place him.

"Sweetheart—" Eden's mother had stepped between them now, clasping her daughter's elbow and steering her toward the sofa "—you remember Rob Peterson, don't you? He lives just down the block."

"Oh...that's right," Eden muttered, accepting the man's proffered handshake as he rose shakily to his feet. There had also been a *Mrs.* Peterson, she remembered now, a plain heavyset woman who'd played the organ in church. And there'd been a couple of Peterson kids, a boy and a girl, close to Eden's own age. Where, she wondered darkly, did her petite lively mother fit into this picture?

"Rob's wife, LuDeen, passed away last fall," Eden's mother interjected as if reading her daughter's mind. "Rob and I, we've been, uh, dating for a couple of months now. I meant to tell you sooner, dear, but somehow I just didn't get around to it. . . ."

Her voice trailed off, crushed by the weight of silence in the room. Rob Peterson shuffled his feet, scarcely able to meet Eden's still-incredulous gaze. He wasn't a bad-looking man, she conceded, taking in his tall thin frame and gaunt features. But he did seem awfully shy.

"Have you eaten, dear?" Eden's mother flitted toward the kitchen. "I've got a Jell-O cake in the fridge. Or I can warm up some leftover chicken divan from Sunday. It should still be—"

"Don't worry about it, Mom." Eden sighed as she stooped to gather up her dropped bags. "I'm too tired to eat. What I really need is a shower and a good night's rest. We can visit tomorrow in the car." She stumbled toward the stairs, intending to make a return trip for the Pullman, which was still on the porch. "Oh...nice meeting you again, Mr. Peterson. Please don't let me spoil your evening."

"Hold on there, young lady. I'll help you with those!" Rob Peterson had finally stirred to life. He snatched Eden's garment bag from her hand, then retrieved the Pullman from the open doorway and marched upstairs with a heavy suitcase slung under each long arm. Choosing not to follow him for the moment, Eden sank into an armchair.

"I'm sorry, Mom," she said lamely. "If I'd had any idea..."

"It wasn't your fault, dear." Eden's mother fluttered around the room like a nervous little finch, plumping cushions and flicking away imaginary dust. "I should have told you about Rob and me. At least that way, you wouldn't have been so shocked."

"I wasn't—"

"Yes, you were. If you'd had false teeth, they'd have dropped right out of your mouth— Oh, sweetheart!" She plopped onto the ottoman and seized Eden's hand in her warm trembling fingers. "I'm fifty-two years old, Eden. Your father's been gone twenty years, and I've been so alone, so lonely. Don't begrudge me this little bit of happiness."

"Mom, it's not that I begrudge you anything. It's just..." Eden struggled for the right words. "It's just going to take a little while for the surprise to wear off, that's all." She glanced toward the still-empty staircase. "He really does seem like a nice man."

"Oh, I knew you'd like him! We—" Eden's mother broke off at the sound of a creaking step. "Be a dear and give us a few minutes to say good-night," she whispered, leaning closer. "We won't be seeing each other again till after the surgery, and I know poor Rob's a lot more worried than he lets on. His wife, bless her, died on the operating table, and he's so afraid the same thing might happen to me..."

She turned a vibrant smile on the lanky man moving awkwardly down the stairs. *Why, she's in love!* Eden realized with a jolt of awareness. *My sensible, levelheaded mother is in love!*

At the sight of her, Rob Peterson's long-jawed face softened in rapt adoration. Eden suppressed a groan. Tomorrow, after a good night's rest, she might be ready to deal with this new development. But not tonight. Not while she was raw-eyed, bone-tired and still reeling from her encounter with Travis Conroy.

The moonstruck lovers seemed to have eyes only for each other. This was definitely not a good time to hang around making small talk.

Shouldering her work-crammed briefcase, Eden murmured her good-nights and trudged upstairs to the bliss of the waiting shower.

Half an hour later, damp and scrubbed, she sat cross-legged on the bed in her old chenille robe. After her frenetic day, she had fully expected to crash on the pillow and sleep like death, but it wasn't happening. She was wide awake, her body pumping adrenaline, her nerves jangling as if she'd overdosed on Forty-second Street espresso.

Except for the hiss of the neighbor's sprinkler through the open window, the house was oppressively quiet. Eden's mother had gone off somewhere with Rob in the car, cheerily telling her daughter not to wait up. And that was all right, Eden told herself. After so many lonely years, her mother deserved some romance in her life. All the same, she couldn't help feeling as if the world had flip-flopped and she had suddenly become Madge Harper's parent.

Eden's restless gaze prowled the tiny bedroom, which had changed little since she was in high school. Her old dresses still hung in the closet. Her collection of plush animals—pandas, elephants, even a purple cow with a tiny plastic udder—spilled over the arms of the wooden rocker that had belonged to her grandmother. Her books crowded the shelves.

If she had time this month, Eden resolved, she would clean out the room and get rid of everything, down to the furniture. And why not? The clothes were hopelessly out of style. The toy animals would amuse some needy children. As for the books, even her high school yearbooks...

Eden's thoughts sputtered and stalled as her gaze fell on the four red-and-white editions of the South Sevier High School *Symbolon.* She should have thrown them out, she berated herself. She should have burned them. But she had not. Now there they sat—graphic reminders of a time she wanted only to forget.

Unbidden, her hand reached out and tugged the oldest most battered yearbook from its place on the shelf. As she balanced it spine-down, the pages fell open at the Athletics section. Only then did she remember how she'd slept with the open book under her pillow.

Get it over with, you idiot! Bemoaning her weakness, she opened the volume flat on her lap and resigned herself to looking.

There he was—Travis Conroy, in his basketball uniform, the first year he'd made the Class A All-State team. He'd also been Junior Class vice president, she recalled, and Junior Class preferred man.

Travis Conroy, golden, gifted and totally beyond her reach.

Eden stared at the photograph, her spirit cringing now at the memory. How many hours had she spent gazing at that picture, burning its image into her foolish young brain? How many times had her eyes traced his signature, with the brief line he'd scrawled when she'd asked him so tremulously to sign her book?

To Edna Rae. Believe in yourself. Best wishes, Travis Conroy.

Believe in yourself. Eden snapped the book shut and shoved it back into place. She had read that message over and over, repeating it like a mantra until it became part of her. Belief in herself had gotten her through college. It had taken her to New York, to a position in the office of a major publisher.

And Travis had probably written the same trite words in every high-school yearbook he signed!

Yearbook.

High school.

Oh, no!

Eden groaned as she remembered the upcoming three-class reunion. The invitation had arrived at her apartment six weeks ago, dutifully forwarded by her mother. Eden had tossed it into the trash, thanking her stars that she would be safely in New York when the event took place. Now, with her mother's surgery and month-long recovery period, she would be right here in town.

Not that she would ever go. Chinese water torture would be preferable to spending an evening with two hundred people who remembered Edna Rae. But she would be *expected* to go. There would be pressure from—

The phone shrilled from the first-floor hallway, shattering her train of thought. She bolted out of the room. Maybe it was her mother. Maybe something had gone wrong with—

"Hello?" The race down the stairs had left her breathless.

"Do you always pant like that when you answer the phone?" The deep warm voice curled like smoke in her ear.

"Travis?" She blinked indignantly.

"I hope I didn't wake you," he said.

"No." She made an effort to sound annoyed. "What is it?"

"Sorry to call so late. I've got something of yours. Something you might like returned."

"What?" Eden's mind had gone blank.

"How about your jacket?"

"Oh . . . that's right."

"Nicole's down for the night. I managed to liberate the jacket before I poured her into bed. Since you're driving your mother north tomorrow, I thought you might like to have it back before then." He paused for a tick of anticipatory silence. "As long as you're still awake, why don't I run by and drop it off?"

Eden's pulse erupted in a maddening skitter of panic. "Oh, that's a lot of trouble for you—"

"Look, it's a ten-minute drive, and there'll be no better time to give you the jacket. Anyway, I've got some unwinding to do before bedtime. See you in fifteen or so, all right?"

"Travis—"

"Don't worry, I won't plan on staying long." The line clicked and went dead.

Eden's head clunked dismally against the wall. Someone had rewritten her script, and nothing was turning out the way she'd expected. Just when she'd managed to convince herself that *she* was in charge of her life, the other characters had started inventing their own lines. First her mother. Now Travis.

And he would be knocking on her door in less than fifteen minutes.

Awakening suddenly to her dripping hair, scrubbed face and faded bathrobe, Eden wheeled and sprinted upstairs. Her Pullman case, hastily dumped, yielded a pair of well-worn jeans and a lavender polo shirt. Jerking them on, she slicked her fine blond hair with mousse and combed it back off her face. Her makeup was—

But what was she doing? The man was coming by to return her jacket, for heaven's sake, and here she was, fluttering around as if they were going to the Russian Tearoom! No. No makeup.

Eden glanced at her pale bare face in the mirror. Without makeup, she looked like Little Orphan Annie. Worse, even, she looked like Edna Rae.

But no matter. It was almost ten o'clock, she was ready for bed, and she was not putting on her face just to impress Travis Conroy. She swung resolutely away from the mirror as the doorbell rang.

Pausing long enough to jam her feet into comfortable brown loafers, she ran—no, walked slowly, with studied indifference—down the stairs to open the front door.

"Hi." Travis had the jacket slung over his left arm. He looked tired, she thought. He looked as if he would rather be home in bed. For that matter, he looked as if he would rather be almost anywhere than here, standing on the porch, talking to Edna Rae Harper.

"Hi." Eden tried to sound casually polite. "Uh, would you like to come in? My mother said something about a Jell-O cake in the fridge."

Travis's face mirrored his hesitation. "Is your mother still up? I wouldn't want to disturb her."

Or to be alone with me, Eden theorized. Maybe he was afraid she was going to lure him into the house and seduce him. With Jell-O cake, no less.

"Actually my mother isn't even here," she said, a raw note creeping into her voice. "My mother is out on a ... date!"

"Oh." One thick black eyebrow tilted knowingly. "With Mr. Peterson, I take it."

Eden slumped against the doorframe. "So the whole town knows. And I don't find out until I walk in and catch them necking on the couch."

"Hey!" Travis's dimples deepened with ill-suppressed amusement. "So your mom's human. It happens to the best of us, kiddo."

"Oh, it's not that." Eden scuffed at the doorframe with the toe of her shoe, feeling clumsy and inadequate. "I just wish she'd let me know sooner. I *am* her daughter, after all."

"Maybe that's just why she *didn't* let you know. Maybe she was afraid you wouldn't feel comfortable about it." He paused to loop Eden's linen jacket over the doorknob. "I think I'll pass on the Jell-O cake, thanks. But you sound like you could use a stroll around the block with Uncle Travis."

Eden's heart slammed into her throat. "What about—"

"Look, it's pitch-dark out here and everybody's inside watching Jay Leno. Come on, it'll do you good to talk."

Eden's resistance crumbled as he punctuated his words with a persuasive tug at her elbow. Maybe it would be all right. Maybe a walk in the cool night air would be just what she needed after the nerve-jangling day.

Travis's pickup, she noticed, was parked discreetly across the street in the shadow of a huge yellow rose thicket. Had he purposefully avoided leaving the vehicle in front of her house? But why wonder? The merest trickle of gossip could swell to a wave that would wash up the old scandal like a corpse on a riverbank. It was the last thing either of them wanted.

"Maybe this isn't such a good idea," she said, forcing herself to resist.

"Come on." He was already moving rapidly down the drive, steering her along beside him. Eden lengthened her stride to keep from stumbling as they fled the glare of the porch light and turned down the darkened sidewalk. Beside her, his body was tense, his grip on her elbow gently compelling.

"You can let me go," she muttered, matching her step to his. "I promise I won't run screaming into the night."

He released her arm with a wry chuckle, probably thinking that *he* was the one who should consider running. But his pace slowed where the light melted into shadow. For a few moments they drifted along in uneasy silence, Travis watching the moon, Eden staring down at her feet. Crickets chirped in the weeds along the old ditch, their songs quivering in the night.

How many times had she fantasized this scene, with the two of them alone in the sweet summer darkness? How many times had she pictured them walking together, imagined him drawing her into the shadows and taking her in his arms?

"So tell me about my mother and Mr. Peterson," she ventured as they headed south toward the corner where a hundred-year-old cottonwood, planted by pioneer settlers, towered against the stars. "I'd like to know at least as much as the rest of the town seems to."

"There's not much to tell." Travis thrust his hands into his pockets as if he did not know what else to do with them. "Rob's a decent sort. Works for the BLM out of Richfield. His kids have grown up and left, so I guess Rob's been pretty lonesome since LuDeen died."

"Uh-huh." Eden stared at the sidewalk and thought of her warm vivacious mother in Rob Peterson's arms. "It sounds serious, doesn't it?" she murmured, swallowing self-consciously.

"I'd judge it to be." Travis paused at the corner to gaze up into the branches of the ancient cottonwood. The night was a symphony of seductive sounds—the rustle of leaves in the soft evening wind, the plaintive song of a cricket, the hiss of a lawn sprinkler. From up the street, the sweet wild scent of yellow roses perfumed the darkness.

"Would it be all that bad? Think how long your mother's been alone. You must want more than that for her."

"Oh, I do!" she answered almost too quickly. "I want my mother to be happy. It's just..."

"Just what?" He was standing so close she could hear the soft rasp of his breathing. His skin radiated heat, as if he had kept the sunlight inside him. Eden's heart broke into an erratic canter.

*This is insane! Travis can't stand me! Just being this close
probably makes his flesh crawl!*

"I . . . I just don't want my mother to be hurt, that's all,"
she stammered.

"Hurt? You mean, like you've been hurt?"

Eden's breath jerked as if he had struck her. "I don't
know what you're talking about!"

He glanced down, his eyes hidden in shadow. "I, uh, ran
into your mother in the post office a few months ago. She
said something about flying back East for your wedding,
and now—"

Travis broke off, realizing, perhaps, that he had said too
much.

"And now, here I am, ringless and manless." Eden finished the sentence for him, her words edged with the bitter-
ness she had not quite been able to shed. "All right, you
might as well know. The wedding was ten days off. I had the
invitations mailed, the food ordered, the gown paid for..."
She sighed raggedly. "He changed his mind. He simply
called me at work one morning and said he couldn't go
through with it. I . . . sent his ring back by express messen-
ger and never saw him again."

"Sounds like you're better off without him."

"That's what I try to tell myself. Chet was a jerk. But at
least he was an honest jerk. If he'd swallowed his reserva-
tions and gone through with it . . ." Eden bit back the rest,
embarrassed by the tremor in her voice.

"It hurts all the same, doesn't it?" Travis asked in what
Eden recognized as a pat-you-on-the-back tone.

*He's putting on a front, trying to be nice, that's all. He's
patronizing me.*

"Uh-huh." She exhaled sharply, forcing the memory to
the back of her mind. "Hey, I thought it was my mother we
were talking about."

"Was it?" Travis's feigned blank look melted into a
knowing sigh. "All right, enough playacting. Something's

been chewing on you all day. I can feel it every time you look at me."

"It doesn't matter anymore." Eden turned away, but he caught her arm, pulling her back into the shadows. Her heart stopped as his head bent breathlessly close. Then, as if catching himself, he drew back.

"It matters. Out with it, lady."

"All right." She glared up at him, quivering with the awareness of how wise he must feel, how superior to dumb little Edna Rae Harper. "I didn't know how much trouble I caused you until today, when Nicole said something about that stupid letter incident."

"Nicole knows?" Surprise flashed across his face.

"Oh, she doesn't know the details. And she doesn't know it was me. But she heard the story from a friend just last summer. People still talk about what happened, Travis. People still remember."

"Come on. You were just a silly kid, and it was a long time ago."

"Was it?" Eden felt the frustration erupting inside her. "That letter haunted me all through high school, Travis. It's going to take all the nerve I can muster just to show my face in this hidebound unforgiving little town!"

"Don't blame the town, Eden."

She stared up at him, dry-mouthed and trembling. Deep inside her, a small voice whispered that he was right, but her pride would not listen. She groped for something to say, something that would sound flip and sophisticated, as if she didn't care. But nothing emerged except a small tense whisper.

"If you're waiting for an apology, I offered you one at the airport. Goodbye, Travis. Thank you for the ride."

Eden's racing heartbeat echoed in her ears as she turned and stalked away, battling the urge to break into a run. The fantasy was over once and for all, she told herself. It was time to face the truth. In this town, Travis would always be the golden boy. And she would always be Edna Rae.

From somewhere in the darkness came the sound of a screen door opening and a woman's voice calling a cat. Eden strode faster, her hands thrust hard into the pockets of her jeans. As she reached the porch, she heard the sound of Travis's pickup growling away from the curb.

She did not turn around to watch it go.

Chapter Four

Travis exhaled raggedly as he pulled the truck onto the main road. Glancing at the speedometer, he forced his foot to ease up on the gas pedal. With everything else that had gone haywire today, the last thing he needed was a speeding ticket.

He swore under his breath as the gears ground into high, his senses recalling the delicious torture of groping between Eden's knees for the shift knob. If the lady had realized what her nearness was doing to him, she probably would have jumped out of the truck and run screaming into the sagebrush.

Blast her—Eden or Edna Rae, or whoever she was tonight! He had almost kissed her there in the shadows of the big cottonwood. She had seemed so soft, so vulnerable and in need of comfort that his male instincts had surged like a hot spring tide. If she hadn't gone skittish on him . . .

But what was he thinking? Eden had done him a big favor by bolting off into the darkness. Taking her in his arms would have been an invitation to disaster!

The weather-beaten pickup growled up the long slope of the Joetown Hill, then swung left onto the side road that led to the ranch. The night was dark, the sky spattered with stars. A jackrabbit flashed across the gravel road, a bounding shape in the headlights. The night was beautiful, but lonely. Too damned lonely.

If he had any sense, Travis lectured himself, he would forget he'd ever set eyes on Eden Harper. He would go home and call up Donetta Ferguson, who had brought him a batch of peanut-butter fudge last week, and invite her out for pizza and a movie tomorrow night.

That wouldn't be a bad idea—except that Nicole was here now. And even if she wasn't, it would take a major effort to work up much interest in Donetta Ferguson—especially after the long ride home with the disquieting Miss Harper.

Travis's thoughts scattered like buckshot as he rumbled through the open chain-link gate and pulled up to the house. He was sure he'd turned off the kitchen light, but now he saw it was on. Nicole must have awakened and found the note he'd stuck on the fridge. At least, he hoped she'd found it. Otherwise, she might be anxious about where her dad had gone.

He switched off the engine, troubled by a vague sense that something was wrong. And it wasn't just the light. The dogs were missing, too. Boss, the aging collie, and Benny, the young black Lab, usually came trotting out to meet him. But tonight there was no sign of them. The yard was empty all the way to the white-painted paddock fence.

Swinging down from the cab, he stiffened warily as an out-of-place odor, faint but unmistakable, pricked his nostrils.

Cigarette smoke.

Someone had been here. Maybe even—

Panic seized Travis's heart as he charged up the steps. If some sleazy drifter had come by and found Nicole alone...

Frantic, he burst through the front door. He charged through the living room and into the spacious, old-fashioned kitchen.

Nicole was seated at the table in her nightgown and robe, sipping a Diet Coke. The sugary remains of a chocolate-glazed doughnut lay scattered on the red-checked vinyl cloth. The two dogs slept at her feet. Benny thumped his tail as Travis approached. Boss did not stir.

"Hi, Daddy." Nicole rested her chin on her palm, her liquid brown eyes gazing up at him. "You look funny. Are you all right?"

Travis's knees had gone watery with relief. Shaking, he slumped onto a chair. "You, uh, didn't notice anybody outside a while ago, did you?"

"Uh-uh. Why?"

"Nothing." No sense scaring her. He was here now, and everything was all right. "Sorry I wasn't around, honey," he apologized. "I know we haven't had much time together, but I thought you were down for the night."

"It's okay. I saw your note." She took a long swig from the red-and-white can.

"That stuff'll keep you awake."

"So?" She took another sip. "You like Eden, don't you?"

"I scarcely know her. She's changed a lot since high school."

Nicole picked up a crumb of chocolate icing from the tablecloth and placed it daintily on the tip of her tongue. "I think Eden's cool. It kicks that a girl from this dumb little town could go off to New York and make something of herself."

"A lot of folks from this town have made something of themselves, Nicole. I've known people from Monroe who became doctors, judges, college professors—"

"Maybe you ought to ask her out."

Travis's mind lurched as he scrambled for an answer. "There's . . . not much future in that," he managed to say. "Eden's going back to New York as soon as her mother's up and around."

"So? Did I say you had to marry her?"

"Besides," he added, ignoring her comment, "I've already got a best girl for the summer, and she's sitting right here."

"Oh, please!" Nicole's withering glance told him what she thought of his comment. "You need a life, Daddy!"

Travis swallowed a sharp prickle of annoyance. "For your information, young lady, I *have* a life, and you're a very important part of it. So, what do you say we both get some sleep? We'll get up early tomorrow, take the horses up the canyon and see if the fish are biting."

Nicole groaned.

"Come on now." Travis eased out of his chair, struggling to ignore the dismay that had settled like a lead weight in his chest. "Things will look better after a good night's rest, I promise." He came around the table and bent swiftly down to kiss the top of her head, then froze in midmotion.

The smoky odor he'd noticed outside clung to his daughter's silky dark curls.

"Nicole, what the—?"

She moved fast, upsetting her Coke can as she jerked to one side. The clear brownish liquid fizzed onto the tablecloth, dripping off the edge and into her lap.

Still in shock, Travis reacted automatically. Grabbing a dish towel off the countertop, he began sponging at her soggy nightclothes.

"It's no problem, Daddy." Nicole twisted away from him. "I can . . ." Her words ended in a whimper as Travis's fingers encountered a partly mashed rectangular object in the left pocket of her robe.

The towel dropped to the floor as he took a step away from her, fighting for self-control.

"All right, Nicole, hand it over," he demanded in a flat voice.

At least she knew better than to argue. Her small hand trembled as she reached into her pocket and drew out a damp, misshapen pack of cigarettes with one smoke missing.

"On the table," he said. "Does your mother know you've got these?"

Nicole shook her head wretchedly.

"I want the truth now. Where did you get them?"

"The place where we stopped for snacks this afternoon." Her voice was no more than a whisper. "When I went back in for a toothbrush—"

"Damn it, you're underage! Didn't they check?"

"I...I talked to this guy. Told him they were for you. He bought them for me."

Travis swore under his breath, biting back the urge to seize her shoulders and shake some sense into her. "Go to bed, Nicole," he said coldly. "I'm too angry to deal with you tonight. We'll talk in the morning."

Her brown eyes glittered with tears. "Daddy, I—"

"Go on." Travis kept his voice hard, his expression rigid. "Go on, before I say something we'll both be sorry for."

Nicole needed no more urging. Flashing him one last stricken glance, she snatched up the hem of her bathrobe and bolted for the stairs.

Travis stood like stone as her footsteps faded into silence. Only after the overhead creak of metal springs told him she was truly in bed did he slump onto the chair. For a long time he sat staring at the cigarette pack Nicole had left on the table.

A lot of kids smoked in California, he reminded himself. But Nicole was barely fourteen, far too young to take up such a dangerous habit. Worse, she had deceived him. She had approached a strange man and sweet-talked him into buying cigarettes for her. What else was the little vixen capable of doing?

Desperation tightened like a fist around Travis's heart. His precious little girl, he realized, was well along the road to trouble. Somehow, whatever the cost, he had to find a way to turn her around.

I think Eden's cool....

Nicole's words drifted through his mind like a life preserver floating past a drowning sailor. Eden—maybe she was part of the answer. She was savvy, sophisticated and accomplished, just the kind of role model an intelligent girl like Nicole needed. Even more important, Nicole seemed to like her. Maybe...

Travis stretched toward the wall phone, then stopped himself with a jerk. What was he thinking? Eden Harper had made it clear she didn't want to see him again or be involved in his family problems. Calling her for help would only put her in an awkward position and make him look like a fool. Nicole was *his* responsibility—Eden had said so in as many words. He would have to find another way.

Moving in a red haze of frustration, he crushed the damp cigarette pack in his fist and flung it into the kitchen wastebasket. Then, in an afterthought, he twisted the top of the plastic liner into a knot and hauled it outside to the big trash receptacle. Slowly he walked back to the porch, where the two dogs waited, and crumpled onto the top step.

The night was warm and quiet, the air sweet with sage and alfalfa. Travis inhaled the cool clean fragrance, feeling angry and lonesome and scared. For months he'd looked forward to a carefree summer with his daughter. Now he knew that the weeks ahead would be a battle for Nicole's future happiness. It was a battle he could not afford to lose.

Stroking the dogs, he pondered how desperately he needed someone to fight at his side. But when that someone was Edna Rae Harper—no, he didn't need that kind of trouble. He was crazy even to think about it.

All the same, as he sat and listened to the crickets singing, the face that drifted again and again through his mind
was a delicate porcelain square with a ripe mouth and
forthright hazel eyes, framed by a nimbus of spun-sugar
hair.

Eden sprawled across her rumpled bed, staring up at the
shadows on the ceiling of her old room. Her thoughts swarm
in maddening spirals, refusing to settle into sleep.

How many nights had she lain like this, picturing Travis's face in the darkness above her, imagining his mouth
brushing her forehead, nibbling her closed eyelids, tasting
her eagerly parted lips? How many times had she dreamed
of his hands, exploring her trembling body, caressing her...

*Good heavens! When am I going to stop being a pathetic
little dunce?*

Flopping onto her belly, she gave the pillow a savage
punch and closed her eyes, determined to sleep. But it was
no good. The three-ring circus going on in her head would
not shut down.

Sitting up, she brushed an impatient hand through her
tangled hair. The garish display on the digital alarm clock
read 12:42. Her mother had come home an hour ago,
sneaking up the stairs like a teenager who'd missed curfew.
Eden had pretended not to hear. She loved her mother, but
she was not up to a gushing account of her relationship with
Rob Peterson. Right now, in fact, all she wanted to do was
crawl into a hole somewhere and die!

For perhaps the twentieth time that night, her mind traced
each step, each word, gesture and nuance of her encounter
with Travis Conroy, from the first meeting of their eyes at
the airport to her flustered retreat down the moon-dappled
walk. The sum of the experience was total disaster. Good old
Edna Rae had come through again!

With a little shudder, Eden wrapped her arms around her
knees. As shadows crept across the room, she sat staring out

at the stars through the branches of the big willow tree. From across the street, the scent of yellow roses floated on the late-night breeze. They were as old as the town, those half-wild yellow roses. Tough, gnarly and bristling with thorns, they grew wherever they were allowed, spreading through backlots, spilling over fences and ditches. Most people nowadays looked on them as a nuisance, but their aroma was like nothing else on earth. Even the wood was fragrant, releasing its sweetness when you cut into the spiny canes.

Nothing ever changed in this town, Eden reminded herself bitterly. Travis Conroy was still golden, still perfect. She was still the ugly duckling, and her foolish little heart still did flip-flops every time she looked at him.

Too agitated to sit still, she swung her legs off the bed, took a step toward the door and stubbed her big toe hard on the rocking chair. The pain shot like lightning up her leg. Eden sucked in her breath, hopping up and down as the agony subsided. Then she sank back onto the bed, tears flooding her eyes.

Her toe would recover, she surmised; but the stumble was so like Edna Rae! She couldn't even walk across her own bedroom without tripping over her feet! And tonight with Travis—yes, she'd managed to make a fool of herself every time she opened her mouth. But then, what else could she expect? She had always behaved like an idiot around Travis Conroy, and even after sixteen years, that hadn't changed.

For a little while tonight, Travis had almost appeared to *like* her. But that was only because she'd helped him out with Nicole. He probably thought he owed her a few pleasantries. That, or he'd felt sorry for her.

Well, it didn't make any difference, Eden reminded herself as she stretched out in the bed and jerked the sheet up to her chin. Early tomorrow she would be driving her mother 140 miles north to Provo for tests and surgery. Five days later, they would drive home again. After that she would be too busy with nursing duties to see anyone, least of all Travis Conroy.

Closing her eyes, she forced herself to take long deep breaths. Although her mind was far from relaxed, her body was weary to the bone. Little by little, Eden felt herself drifting on the waves of a half-remembered melody with a throbbing, sensual beat. Lights began to swirl and flicker in her vision as the music flowed through her, its rhythm moving her as gently as water....

Slowly she became aware that there were other people around her, slow-dancing, as she was, amid a swirl of balloons and crepe-paper streamers. Her throat tightened with sudden dread as she realized she was at a high-school dance in the familiar old gym. All around her, she recognized her classmates—Mitzi Cole, the perky cheerleader; LeRoy Hatch, the husky, rugged football captain; Lynette Bartleson, the prom queen, with her long red curls and sophisticated clothes. And the others—all of them golden and glittering, all of them perfect.

Eden's heart fluttered in panic. What was she doing here? She didn't belong. She had never belonged. She had to get away.

Only then did she realize someone was holding her, guiding her in the dance that had become a humiliating ordeal. Her hand rested in a warm leathery palm. Strong fingers cradled the small of her back, pulling her close against a lean muscular body. Travis. She closed her eyes, her anxiety draining away. The feeling was...heaven.

Something moist and satiny brushed her forehead. She whimpered under her breath as the nibbling sensation tingled down her temple and along the curve of her cheekbone. She knew what would come next, and she yearned for it with an urgency that strained her whole body upward, drawn by her hungry seeking lips.

Eden's breath stopped as she felt the sandpapery brush of his chin along her cheek. Then her whole being flash-flamed under the heat of his kiss. She moaned out loud, arms sliding around his neck as she gave herself to the wonder of it. The streamers and balloons faded away. The music dimmed, until there was nothing in her world but Travis, nothing but his arms, nothing but the heaven of his warm strong mouth.

Or so she thought, until she heard whoops of laughter all around them. She gasped, shocked by the contempt in Travis's mocking grin.

"What's the matter, Edna Rae," he drawled, "isn't this what you've always wanted?"

She twisted away from him, aware, suddenly, of her shapeless brown sweater and baggy skirt, of her too-oily hair caught back in a plastic clip, of her face, bare of makeup except for the scattered dots of zit cream that were too dark for her fair skin.

The dancers surrounded her, laughing in a chorus of hoots, guffaws, catcalls and giggles. "Stop it!" she groaned, struggling to break out of their circle. "Stop it! Leave me alone. Please—"

The shrill *beep beep beep* of the alarm clock jarred Eden awake, shattering the dream like a glass Christmas ornament. She groped for the snooze button, hit it, then sat huddled in the darkness, knees drawn up against her chest, eyes staring at the gray streak of dawn outside the window. She felt raw, as if she had scarcely slept at all. But it was five-thirty in the morning. She'd been dead to the world for hours, and it was time to get up.

Through the wall, she could hear her mother, awake and stirring. Eden yawned and slid her feet to the floor. It was time she got moving, too, if they were to make it to Provo by nine. At least the early-morning drive would be cool and free of traffic.

After running a comb through her hair, she rummaged in her suitcase for a pair of white denim jeans and a chambray shirt. The dream was fading from her mind now. Still,

Eden's hands trembled as she hooked her bra and slid her arms into the blue cotton shirtsleeves.

Forget it, she lectured herself. *A dream is just your brain cleaning house, sweeping out the dust and cobwebs so they won't trouble you anymore.*

But what scary dust! What disturbing cobwebs! Travis's dream kiss had seared her to the soles of her feet. And as for the rest—

"I'm finished in the bathroom, dear," her mother's cheery voice warbled through the closed door. "Hurry up. As soon as I'm dressed, I'll run downstairs and make you some coffee and cinnamon toast."

"Thanks." Eden padded down the hall and into the bathroom. Her eyes, reflected in the mirror above the basin, looked as if she'd been on a bender. She splashed cold water on her face, then leaned closer to insert her contact lenses.

How would it *really* feel to kiss Travis? she wondered as she maneuvered one tiny, clear lens into position. But why was she asking herself such a stupid question? She would rather eat poached rattlesnake than kiss Travis Conroy, and he probably felt the same way about her!

But how *would* it feel? Awkward? Ordinary? Thrilling? Lost in thought, Eden leaned closer to the mirror, then muttered a curse as the slippery lens dropped into the basin.

What was the matter with her? she lashed herself as she rescued the lens with a cautious fingernail. She was a grown woman now, not some dippy high-school sophomore. And Travis was no longer the basketball star. He was a man who had never ventured far from his roots, never taken on the challenge of going out in the world to make something of himself. What on earth would she want with a man like that? And why, for that matter, was she even wondering?

What was wrong with her this morning?

"Can I put your toast in now, dear?" Her mother called from the foot of the stairs.

Eden popped the lens into place. "It's okay!" she shouted back. "I'll do it when I come down!"

"You'll be waiting on me hand and foot when we get back!" Madge Harper retorted spunkily. "Let me do something for you while I'm still able!"

"No arguing with you, is there?" Eden rinsed her teeth and swiped a dash of lipstick across her mouth. She could do the rest of her makeup later when she had more time, but right now she didn't want to keep her mother waiting.

Twenty minutes later, they were on the road, the green Buick ripping along the two-lane highway that connected the local state road with Interstate 70. Eden drove with the window down, the chilly morning breeze buffeting her hair.

"I never did ask you how you got home last night," her mother remarked in a conversational tone that didn't fool Eden for a second. "Did somebody give you a ride?"

"Travis Conroy. He was at the airport picking up his daughter," Eden answered in a flat voice, hoping the reply would sound nonchalant.

"Travis Conroy. Hmm. I thought I recognized the sound of that old pickup. You can hear it coming three blocks away. With the savings that man's got piled up in the bank, you'd think he'd buy a new truck."

"Uh-huh. So, how was your date with Rob?" Eden groped desperately for a different subject—any subject. "Did you go someplace interesting?"

"We just...talked." Madge Harper trailed off into a pensive silence.

"Mom? Is anything wrong?"

"Watch your speed, dear. There's a patrolman who likes to hide out just past those old sheds. Marian Winkle got a ticket from him last week. She was telling me at club—"

"Mom, I asked you a question. Is something wrong?"

"Wrong?" Eden's mother gave a nervous little laugh. "Why, yes, but not with me, dear. It's *you* I'm worried about."

"Me?" Eden felt as if she were shrinking to the size of a ten-year-old. "Mom, I'm fine. I'm perfectly happy—"

"Rubbish! Look at you!"

"Hey—" Eden tried to pull off a fake grin "—give me a break! It's six-thirty in the morning, and I'm not exactly super-model material."

"That's not what I'm talking about. Ever since you broke up with Chet—"

"Mom, I didn't break up with Chet. Chet dumped me like an overripe sardine sandwich. I guess I wasn't enough woman for him." Eden gunned the car up the Elsinore on-ramp, wishing her mother had chosen to talk about the weather. Or the world population crisis. Or the national debt. "Who knows?" she added, rubbing salt in her own wound. "Maybe I'm not enough woman for any man."

"See what I mean, dear?" Eden's mother sighed. "You're always being too hard on yourself. Maybe you just haven't found the one who's man enough for *you*."

"Do you have any candidates in mind?" The feigned humor in Eden's voice rang hollow.

"None that you wouldn't reject out of hand. But that's not the point, sweetheart. You're a lovely young woman, and you have so much to give. But I've been concerned about you ever since your engagement broke up. Anyone can see that you're working too hard, not taking care of yourself—"

"Mother, I'm a big girl. I'm dealing with the breakup in my own way, but these things take time."

"Did you love Chet that much?"

"I . . . thought I did. Now I don't know."

"Frankly, I wasn't all that impressed by him."

"What?" Eden swerved to miss a hunk of black tire tread on the freeway.

"Oh, he was good-looking in a priggish sort of way—"

"*Priggish?*"

"And he was smart, and ambitious—anyone could see at. But he seemed so focused on himself, Eden—*his* ca-er, *his* plans, *his* preferences—"

"Mother, do we have to have this discussion *now?*"

"Why not?" Madge Harper chuckled. "It's not often I ave you as a captive audience these days!"

Eden groaned good-naturedly. "Then will you please get the point?"

"All right. When am I going to see you happy?"

Eden's jaw went slack as the question struck her like a gut unch. Her mother had always been outspoken, but until ow, her directness had been tempered with tact. Now it was if charming Madge Harper had just yanked off her kid oves.

"Mother, what's gotten into you this morning?" Eden urted.

"Well, you told me to get to the point." Madge smoothed ut a crease in her slacks.

"But did you have to make it such a *sharp* point? I'm appy enough. Just because I'm not married—"

"Did I say anything about marriage?"

"You didn't have to. I know all your friends have grand-ildren. I know you'd love some of your own. I know you ink that all I have to do is find the right man, and every-ing else will fall into place."

"Not at all, dearest." Madge reached over and patted her aughter's knee. "I've lived too long to be that naive. But ere's something I've learned. You set yourself up for appiness or unhappiness. You have to be *ready* when mething good comes along. You have to reach out and tch it before it slips away—"

"Mom, I'm going to be fine," Eden broke in with a little uff of exasperation. "Now, no more lectures, okay? I love ou, but's too early in the morning." She reached for the radio button and clicked it on, hoping for the distraction of a local news broadcast, but nothing came out through the speakers except an annoying blast of static. She punched the select buttons. Nothing—unless you counted a country-and-western station crackling out a growly rendition of "A Woman of Mine." Eden sighed and switched the radio off again.

"So, tell me about your ride south with Travis Conroy," Madge chirped into the silence.

Out of the frying pan and into the fire!

"There's not much to tell," Eden hedged. "His daughter did most of the talking, and I went to sleep. I slept most of the way home."

"Did you now?"

"Stop that, Mom!" Eden kept her eyes on the road, hoping the furious blush that had flooded her cheeks didn't show. "You know I'll never feel at ease around Travis. And he'll never be comfortable around me. He offered me a ride out of politeness, that was all, and I accepted against my better judgment. The whole experience was so awkward we were both relieved when it was over!"

And that was true, as far as it went, Eden rationalized. Tell her mother the full story, and the woman would pounce on it like a cat on fresh mackerel.

"How long has that man been single now? Nine years? Ten?"

"I wouldn't know," Eden snapped, "and I certainly didn't ask him."

Madge fumbled in her handbag for a tissue and blew her nose with a dainty little sniff. "I'd swear half the ladies in the county have set their caps for him at one time or another. Heavens, if I were twenty years younger, I might have gone after the big handsome hunk myself!"

"Mother!" Eden's face was a fiery blaze.

"Some of those women would have made lovely wives. I truly don't know what the man is waiting for."

"Well, at least I can shed some light on that question," den volunteered. "According to his daughter, Travis hasn't married because he's still in love with her mother."

"With Diane?" Madge's tongue clicked in disbelief. "Oh, can't imagine that! Travis's little girl might *want* to be- ve he still loves her mother, but it can't be true. Diane onroy was a very attractive woman, but she hated Mon- e and everything in it. When Travis wouldn't leave, she ad-mouthed him all over town. Finally she went home to sit her family—that's where she got involved with the man e eventually married. Travis was bitter, but I can't imag- e he was all that sorry to see her go."

"So where did you learn all this?" Eden feigned an un- terested shrug.

"From Marvella Johnson, of course. She's been doing my air for fifteen years, and she also does Janice Woodard, ho's married to Travis's cousin Bert and—"

"Never mind! I get the picture!" Eden shook her head sparagingly. "The place is one big gossip mill."

"Oh, you're being too harsh now, dear. It's not gossip in e vicious sense. People care about each other, that's all. 'e like to know what's going on in each other's lives. If yone ever needs help—"

"I know. Casserole City."

"You've been living in New York too long, sweetheart." ladge patted her daughter's knee again. "Now, if you'll xcuse me, I think I'll try a little nap. It's going to be a very ng day." She pulled a small pillow out of the tote bag at er feet, scrunched it between the seat back and the win- w and curled up with her head in the corner. Within min- es she was asleep, or doing a decent job of faking it.

Eden groped for her sunglasses in her purse. She slid them a as the sun broke over the eastern mountains amid a glory f rose-gold clouds. The sunrise was so beautiful it made her roat ache. Keeping one eye on the road, she watched it

glow, then fade, moment by moment, into the blue of a
ordinary morning.

You have to be ready when something good comes along
You have to reach out and catch it before it slips away.

How many sunrises had she missed in her life? Ede
mused idly. How many beautiful experiences had passed he
by because she wasn't ready for them?

Oh, what was the matter with her this morning? Wh
couldn't she think straight? She needed to be back in Ne
York, back at her desk, safe and secure behind a huge stac
of manuscripts. In New York, she was Eden Harper, coo
competent and sure of herself. Here in Utah, she was sui
of nothing, least of all her own identity as a woman.

Had her mother been pushing her at Travis? Had th;
been the thrust of her unusual ploy this morning?

But what a joke! Travis was no more interested in her tha
she was in him! And even if he was—even if he came to he
heart in hand—how could she think of spending her life i
a small town, especially the town where she'd experience
so much humiliation? No, she couldn't even imagine it. Sh
had always wanted a home and family, but not here. Sh
would wither and die in a place like Monroe!

Clutching for something else to occupy her mind, Ede
remembered the briefcase she'd tucked into the trunk of th
car. Work—that was what she needed. As soon as he
mother was settled in, she would get back into some kind o
routine. It was her only hope of staying sane. And if sh
finished the manuscripts she'd brought along, she would ca
Gordon, her assistant at Parnell, and ask him to express
mail her another batch.

As for Mr. Travis Conroy, she had seen the last of him
He could have his ranch and his daughter and his home
spun dreams. He could have the bevy of domestic god
desses who were pursuing him at every turn.

She, for one, had no intention of joining the pack.

Chapter Five

The whole day, Travis reflected darkly, had been one long string of disasters.

To start with, Nicole had refused to get up before eight to go riding. In earlier years he might have dumped her out of bed in a laughing pile of blankets. Now that she was a young woman, however, that tactic no longer seemed appropriate. Instead, he had paced and stewed in the kitchen while her favorite blueberry pancakes dried out and became inedible on the stove.

At eight forty-five she had finally appeared, wearing too much makeup and a pair of jeans so tight she could barely mount her horse. Sullen and silent, she had ridden beside him across the sage flats in the hot morning sun. Travis's feeble attempts at conversation had been like tossing Ping-Pong balls at a brick wall.

They had never made it to the canyon. Tucker, the docile gelding Travis kept for Nicole to ride, had loosened a shoe three miles from the ranch. They had walked the horses home and eaten their packed lunches at the kitchen table.

Travis had thought the worst was over. He was wrong.

After lunch, Nicole had announced she wanted to g
swimming—not at the local hot springs, but at the city po
in Richfield. Travis had acquiesced with relief. Plenty o
kids hung out at the pool. Maybe if his daughter spent son
time with people her own age, she would settle down a li
tle.

He had dropped her off at the pool entrance and drive
downtown to do some errands. An hour later, he'd re
turned to see two police cars, sirens in full cry, pulling int
the parking lot. People were converging on the pool from a
directions.

"What's going on?" he'd demanded, grabbing a teenag
boy by the elbow.

"Fight. Big fight. Two guys started punching it out ove
this girl, and the next thing you know, everybody was jun
pin' into it."

Heart in his throat, Travis had shoved his way to th
chain-link barrier that surrounded the pool area. The figl
was breaking up now that the police had arrived. One husk
high-school boy was nursing a bloody nose. Another wa
slumped beside the pool, splashing water on a badly puffe
eye. Travis had searched frantically for Nicole. Maybe she'
gotten in the way. Maybe she was hurt—

Then he'd spotted her.

She was huddled against the diving-board ladder, her bi
Bambi eyes wide and bewildered, her young golden bod
clad in an orange thong bikini so minuscule it barely co
ered the basics.

"That's her in the orange!" a boy next to him declare
pointing. "That's the girl who started it all!"

The rest of the afternoon had been a blur. He had extri
cated Nicole and driven home in a seething rage that she ha
pretended not to understand.

"But, Daddy," she'd pouted. "*Everybody* wears suits lik
mine in California! I don't see anything wrong with—"

"Be quiet, Nicole," he'd growled. "This is Utah. People tend to be more conservative here. If you want to make friends, you'll need to make an effort to fit in."

"That's not fair! You're asking me to be something I'm not—a phony!"

"What I'm asking you right now is to be quiet!"

Travis's own angry words echoed in his mind as he cleaned up the kitchen and loaded the dishwasher. From Nicole's upstairs room, the sound of the latest rap hit blasted full volume through the ceiling. An hour ago he had left a supper of lasagna and garlic bread outside her closed door. The tray had disappeared, but she had not spoken to him since the ride home.

He should have handled things differently, Travis berated himself. He should have been more patient and encouraged her to talk. Instead, he had condemned his daughter without a hearing. Worse, he had slammed the door on any healing communication between them.

He closed the dishwasher door, then paused, torn by indecision. He could go upstairs, knock on her door and apologize, ask her for another chance—

But he hadn't done anything to apologize *for,* his stern side argued. Caving in now would only weaken his authority and make it easier for her to rebel next time.

He could call Diane in Newport, ask her how she would deal with the situation—

But that wouldn't do, either. The last thing he wanted was to admit to his ex-wife that he couldn't handle his own daughter.

He could find a girlfriend for Nicole, invite her out to the ranch—

But that wasn't as easy as it sounded. In past summers Nicole hadn't made many friends among the local kids. Kim Driscoll, the one girl with whom she'd formed a tentative bond, had moved to Wyoming with her family last fall.

Which left Eden Harper.

Travis stared desperately at the phone. Was it just a co incidence that he'd had business at the BLM and talked with Rob Peterson that afternoon? Was it a coincidence that Rob had mentioned Eden would be staying at the Holiday Inn while her mother was in the hospital—or could it be that he'd steered Rob's conversation along that line? What the hell, maybe it was *fated* that he would call her.

Forcing himself to move, he dialed information and got the phone number for the Holiday Inn. That done, he turned and stared out the window, chewing absentmind edly on his lower lip.

What was he thinking?

Even if he called Eden, what would he say to her? Would he play it cool? Turn on the charm? Throw himself on her sympathy?

And even then, what difference would it make? Eden Harper was one savvy woman. He'd bet good money she wouldn't fall for any of it.

But on the other hand, what if she actually listened? What if she agreed to help? Travis hesitated, still deliberating. No he couldn't call her yet. He needed to reason this out.

Turning away from the phone, he wandered outside onto the shadowy porch. No matter how much he needed Eden it wouldn't be fair, dragging her into his troubles. Sooner o later she would feel used. She would probably end up hat ing him, if she didn't hate him already.

No, it was a crazy idea, bringing her into this. It would never work.

Nicole had finally switched off her music. Travis leaned against the porch railing, listening to the familiar peaceful sounds of evening—the chirping crickets, the horses nick ering in their stalls, the velvet wind whispering through the alfalfa fields. He gazed across the flat to the clustered light of the little town of Monroe, feeling lonesome and frus trated and plain miserable.

The truth was, he wanted to see Eden again for reasons that had nothing to do with Nicole. Damn it, he *liked* Eden. She was intelligent. She was funny. She was as temptingly delicious as warm peach cobbler with homemade ice cream.

He remembered her sexy, breathless little laugh. Suddenly he found himself wanting to hear it again, close enough to tickle his ear this time. He caught himself imagining her in his arms, her curves fitting his embrace as if they'd been molded to him, her baby-silk hair curling soft against his cheek as he found her lips and kissed... nipped... nuzzled...

This was Edna Rae Harper he was fantasizing about, Travis reminded himself. But somehow that reality no longer mattered. He only knew he wanted to see her again, to get to know her as he had never known her in high school.

He would call her, he resolved. He would throw caution to the winds and ask her out. And if the subject of conversation got around to Nicole, fine and dandy. If not, that was all right, too. He would not involve Eden in his family troubles unless she *offered* to become involved. Nicole was *his* problem. He would have to find his own way to influence her.

Bracing his courage, Travis strode to the phone, dialed the hotel number and asked for Eden's room.

The shrilling phone caught Eden stepping out of the shower. Grabbing a towel, she raced across the room, leaving a trail of soggy footprints on the carpet. Maybe it was her mother, or the doctor, or—

She lunged across the bed to catch the receiver in midring. "Hello," she gasped.

"Aha! You *do* pant when you answer the phone." Travis's rich baritone rumbled through the earpiece so clearly he could have been standing beside her. In a self-conscious panic, she jerked the towel against her bare breasts.

"Travis? Is that you?" *Oh, clever response! Way to go, Harper!*

"You were expecting someone else?"

"Uh, no one in particular. How did you know where to call?" Eden punctuated the question with a nervous hiccup. The air-conditioning was on, and her teeth were beginning to chatter.

"You might say I pried the information out of Rob. You sound a little strained. Is this a bad time for you?"

"I'm just, uh, wet, that's all. Hang on, I'll get a robe." She flung the phone on the bed, yanked her black nylon travel robe out of her open suitcase and wrapped it around her shivering body. It didn't take a genius to figure out that Travis wanted some favor from her. Why else would he be sweet-talking her long-distance?

"How's your mother holding up?" The question was a pleasantry, revealing nothing.

"Fine, considering everything. The surgery's scheduled for six tomorrow morning. They've given her something to help her sleep."

"And how are *you* holding up?" His stress on the word "you" triggered a freshet of warmth over the surface of Eden's skin. An image flashed through her mind of Travis cradling the phone against his darkly unshaven jaw, his eyes half-closed in a lazy smile, his lips not quite brushing the mouthpiece. Oh, he knew exactly what he was doing. The man could charm any woman on the planet.

Any woman except *her*, Eden reminded herself with a mental jab.

"I'm fine," she said curtly, "but surely that isn't why you called, is it, Travis?"

The responding tick of silence told her he'd been thrown by her directness. Good. Score one for the klutzy Ms. Harper.

"Uh, no," he said, making a quick recovery. "However, I do have a good excuse for calling you. I'm on the com mittee for the three-class reunion July fifth, and we need a head count by tomorrow night. Did you get your invitation?"

"My invitation?" Eden slumped in her wet black robe as she realized where the conversation was leading. "Oh, yes, my mother saw to that!" She managed a bitter chuckle. "My invitation, or what's left of it, is now the property of the New York City Sanitation Department."

"You're not going?" Travis hesitated, then groaned in mock dismay. "Give me a break, Eden. You've got to go. You'll knock everybody's socks off!"

"No." Eden realized she was shaking her hair like a wet spaniel. She forced herself to stop and take a deep breath before she finished answering him. "Your flattery isn't helping, Travis. I have no desire to go to the reunion and be stared at like a circus freak. I got enough of that in high school, thank you."

Her comment seemed to sober him. "A freak? Is that what you felt like back then?"

"Isn't that the way *you* saw me?" she challenged. "Come on, truth or dare."

His silence lay like winter on the line. Eden waited, wishing she could take the question back, knowing it was too late.

An eternity seemed to pass before he spoke. "To be honest, I hardly saw you at all—not until you came striding out of that jetway like a big, beautiful, confident cat, and—"

"Oh, stop it!" Eden flushed hot beneath her robe. "This is getting silly, Travis. Besides, we're running your phone bill through the ceiling."

"So you think I'm going to let you off the hook that easily, do you?" Travis's cocky manner had returned. He let her squirm as he paused for a long breath. "Tell you what, I'll include you in the count. That way, if you change your mind—"

"I won't change my mind. I'd rather be eaten alive!"

"Now, there's an interesting possibility."

"Are you finished?" Eden's blush had become a crimson blaze.

"Not really. The reunion was just my excuse for tracking you down. Actually I called to apologize."

"Apologize?"

"I got a little too smart for my britches last night. You were right in calling me on it. Thanks."

"Thanks?" She blinked, aware that she sounded about as intelligent as a pet-store parrot.

"I was hoping you'd let me make amends when you get back to Monroe—say, over dinner some night."

Dinner. Eden's throat went dry. Her heart clenched like a fist, then lurched into terminal velocity.

He was asking her for a date.

Travis Conroy was asking her for a date.

"When it comes to dining, I'm aware Sevier County isn't on a par with New York," he was saying. "But I know a little place that serves pretty decent ribs. They've even got an old fifties jukebox, if you like to dance."

An invisible band of fear tightened around Eden's ribs. "I…I never did learn to dance," she stammered. "Not even in college."

"Maybe you just didn't have the right teacher." The warmth in his voice sent her pulse into an intoxicated skitter.

"What…what about Nicole? She just got here. You can't simply go off and leave—"

"Nicole's a big girl. She'll be fine at home with a pizza and a video. So, how about it?"

Eden swallowed hard, telling herself to be sensible. Travis wanted something, and it couldn't be *her*. Time would bear that out, and in the end she would only be hurt again.

"I really don't think that's such a good idea," she hedged. "People will talk, you know."

"Let them talk. What harm can it do? We're both single and over twenty-one."

"Travis, I don't—"

"You're an attractive, intriguing, damned sexy woman, Eden Harper. If wanting to know you better is a crime, then I plead guilty. Go ahead and sue me."

"No, it's not that." Eden struggled against the clashing emotions that threatened to turn her into a tongue-tied fool. "It's my mother. Don't you understand how much she's going to need me? I can't just—"

"Yes or no?"

"I . . . no, I just can't. I'm sorry."

"All right." Travis's breath broke in a ragged sigh as his defenses slid back into place. "I understand how busy you'll be. Hey—the offer's still open if you find yourself free and change your mind."

"Thank you." She would not, could not change her mind, Eden knew. "Uh, how's Nicole?"

"Fine. I'll tell her you asked."

"Tell her I said hello."

"I will." In the silence that hung awkwardly on the line, Eden sensed the strain in him—a strain of words held back, of things he wanted to tell her, and would if she allowed him an opening.

For an instant she hesitated, lips parted, wondering what might happen if she just—

But no, how could she risk it? Travis Conroy would stomp all over her heart, then walk away and not think twice about it. Sixteen years ago, she might have let him, but she was all grown up now. She knew better.

"I have to go," she muttered. "My hair is dripping water all over the bedspread."

"Okay." He sounded relieved, she thought. "Give my best to your mother."

"Thanks. She'll appreciate that. Uh, bye now."

Eden disconnected the call with a trembling forefinger and slipped the receiver into its cradle. Then she sat huddled miserably on the edge of the mattress, aching to dial him back, recant every stupid trite thing she'd said and ask him how he liked his women dressed for dinner.

No, it would never work. A date with Travis might be thrilling, but down the road, she would pay the price in hurt and humiliation.

Better safe than sorry, she reminded herself, dropping her bare feet to the floor and reaching for the towel to wrap her hair. It was over, whatever *it* had been. Travis was a proud man, and he could have his pick of eager pretty women. Why should he bother with Edna Rae Harper?

Eden could not answer that question, but one thing was certain. If ever she'd had a chance with Travis Conroy, she'd just blown it.

He would not be calling her again.

"Daddy?"

The small voice startled Travis as he hung up the phone. He turned to see Nicole huddled at the foot of the stairs in her old patchwork flannel robe, her arms clutching the moth-eaten teddy bear he'd given her for her third birthday. With her face scrubbed bare of makeup, she looked about ten years old.

His heart softened to an aching lump of putty.

"Were you calling Eden?" she asked innocently.

"Uh-huh. I took your advice and asked her out."

"Oh?"

"She said she was busy." Travis hid his dejection with a careless grin. "It looks like you'll have to be my best girl, after all."

"I'll always be your best girl, Daddy." She gave him a melting smile. "But Eden likes you. I know she does. She even told me so."

"Well, the lady seems to have changed her mind." Travis lowered himself onto a chair, savoring the uneasy truce. "Hey, I've got an idea. Why don't we pretend that you just got here, and the past two days never happened? Maybe we can get off to a better start on the second try."

"Okay. Can I have a chocolate doughnut and a glass of milk?"

"Sure. I'll even get them for you." Travis bounded out of the chair, plopped a doughnut onto a clean saucer and poured a brimming glass of milk. "What about tomorrow? If you're up for it, we could drive over to Wayne County and go rock hunting. Remember those great geodes we found a couple of years ago? And that little café with the homemade boysenberry pie?"

Nicole had moved to the table, where she was already wolfing down the doughnut. "Uh...that's kind of what I wanted to talk to you about, Daddy."

Travis eased into the chair opposite her, feeling more cheerful than he had in the past two days. Things were going to work out, after all—with Nicole, at least. "Whatever you want to do is fine with me," he said. "Just name it, honey."

"No kidding? You mean that?" She took a sip of milk, her brown eyes sparkling like root beer above the rim of the glass.

"Would I say it if I didn't? Try me."

"Well..." Nicole stuffed down the last bite of doughnut. "There's this really cool guy I met at the pool. His name's Turk. He's got this kickin' Harley tattoo, and he's sooo buff—" She broke off, realizing her words had taken a wrong turn. "Anyway, he's really nice. He says his cousin's got these new four-wheelers. They're going riding in the foothills tomorrow afternoon, and he—uh, Turk—invited me to come along."

A corner of Travis's world crumbled and broke away. He sagged in his chair, feeling like a world-class fool as he met his daughter's challenging gaze.

She read his hesitation. "Daddy, you said I could. You promised..."

Travis shook his head, knowing, as a father, exactly what he had to say. "I did promise. But it's a promise I've no choice except to break. I'm sorry, Nicole. Fourteen is too young to be tearing around in the hills with strange boys. The answer is no."

He watched helplessly as her expression soured from disbelief to outrage.

"That's not fair!" She flung the words at him. "Stop treating me like a child! I'm not your little girl anymore!"

"Nicole..." He shot her a warning glare, hiding the sting with anger.

"No! Listen to me! When I was a little kid, you were my whole world. We did everything together. But I'm growing up now, and it's not the same. You need to get a life, Daddy! Then maybe I can have a life, too!"

Hurling the teddy bear at his chest, she lunged away from him and raced out the kitchen door. Travis sat in quivering silence as the screen slammed behind her, emotions bleeding out of him as if he'd been shot through the heart.

From outside, the growl of the truck engine shocked him back to awareness. Too late, he remembered leaving the keys in the ignition.

"Nicole!" He charged out onto the porch. "Damn it, you're only fourteen! You can't..."

The words died in his throat as the truck roared down the driveway in low gear, crunched into a concrete-imbedded steel gatepost and shuddered to a stop in a hissing cloud of steam.

"Your mother's in recovery. She's going to be fine." The doctor, still in green surgical garb, wiped a bead of perspiration from his cheek. "I was worried about the cancer, but it hadn't spread beyond the uterus. We got it all."

"Cancer?" Eden's magazine slid from her lap to the floor. "What are you saying? I thought the surgery was routine. I thought it was just..."

"Your mother didn't tell you?"

"No. When can I see her?" Eden was on her feet. "Please, I want to see my mother now!"

"She's still coming out of the anesthesia. Sit tight for a few more minutes. They'll send out a nurse as soon as she's awake."

Weak-kneed and trembling, Eden forced herself back onto the settee as the doctor disappeared down a corridor. Why hadn't she guessed something out of the ordinary was wrong with her mother? Why hadn't she picked up on any of the signals—Rob Peterson's concern, Madge's uncharacteristic lecture in the car? How could she have been so blind? Was it because she'd been so preoccupied with Travis that she couldn't think of anything else?

Tears blurred her eyes. It didn't matter anymore, she reminded herself. Her mother was going to be fine now—the doctor had said so. But what if things had gone the other way? What if the cancer had spread?

Unable to sit still, she got up and strode across the waiting room to the window, where she stared out at the cultivated beds of pink petunias and flame red geraniums.

What kind of daughter had she been, living in New York, coming home maybe once a year? Her mother had devoted half a lifetime to raising her. What kind of gratitude had she shown for such a sacrifice?

It was selfish on her part, staying in New York when there were other places, other jobs. Oh, she could never be happy in a small town like Monroe, but Salt Lake City might not be so bad. Finding work shouldn't be a problem for someone with her writing, editing and computer skills. Once she

got settled and bought her own car, she could drive down
and see her mother every couple of weeks.

Yes, the idea was making more and more sense. Eden
paced the length of the room, her mind churning. Madge
Harper had been alone long enough. All that was going to
change—yes, it would even be fun! They could go to plays
and concerts together, maybe drive to the Shakespeare Fes-
tival in Cedar City next summer, or—

"Miss Harper?" The nurse's crisp voice made Eden start.
"Your mother's awake now and asking for you. You can see
her for a few minutes. Just follow me."

Eden hurried along the corridor. Her throat tightened as
they swung through the recovery-room door and a second
nurse drew aside one of the blue-striped curtains that sepa-
rated the patients.

"Mom?"

The figure in the bed looked disturbingly small and quiet.
But no—it was all right. Madge Harper's bright blue eyes
were open. Her face wore a tired smile.

"Hello, dear," she murmured sleepily.

"Why didn't you tell me?" Eden gripped her mother's
thin cool hand. "Why didn't you tell me it was cancer?"

"And upset you over nothing? Whatever for? I'm going
to be fine. The doctor says I'll probably live to be ninety."

"You told Rob, didn't you? That's why he seemed so
worried."

"Rob needed to know. There was a reason for it. You
see . . ." Madge's clasp tightened around her daughter's fingers. A soft radiance warmed her face. "Rob asked me to
marry him two weeks ago. I told him that my answer would
depend on the outcome of this operation."

Eden blinked at her, dazed by the news. "Mother, are you
sure this is—"

"Oh, stop being so sensible, sweetheart!" Madge was
beaming now from ear to ear. "Tell me, what would you say
to being a September bridesmaid?"

Chapter Six

Madge Harper's homecoming was a full-scale social event.

Not that Eden had planned it that way. She had hoped to smuggle her mother quietly in through the side door, tuck her into bed and let her doze undisturbed for the rest of the afternoon. But it was not to be.

Rob Peterson had appeared on the front porch within minutes, his Lincolnesque face a landscape of smiling creases. In his pocket he'd carried a velvet box. When his big awkward hands slipped the tiny diamond engagement ring onto Madge's finger, seeing them together had been like looking into sunlight.

Awash in emotion, Eden had excused herself and rushed off to the kitchen to make fresh lemonade. Five minutes later the ringing doorbell had announced Ella Skidmore with a pan of fresh, hot potato rolls and LaVerne Filstrup with a lime-Jell-O salad.

For the next hour, Eden rushed back and forth, answering the door, serving lemonade with the oatmeal cookies someone else had brought and generally making an effort to stay out of people's way. Luckily Madge's diamond was causing such a furor that nobody paid her much heed. Still, it was only by chance that she happened to look out the window and see a small forlorn figure sitting cross-legged on the front lawn.

"Nicole?" She opened the door and stepped out onto the porch.

"Hi." Nicole glanced back over her shoulder. She was wearing cutoffs, a yellow No Fear T-shirt and sandals. Her suntanned legs were streaked with dust. There was no sign of Travis or the truck.

"Uh, what a surprise!" Eden managed to exclaim. "How did you get here?"

"Walked."

"All the way from the ranch?" Eden had pedaled the distance often enough to know it was a good four miles.

"Uh-huh," Nicole murmured. "All the way from the ranch."

"You must be hot. Would you like to come inside?"

"No, thanks. You seem to have plenty of company."

"It's my mother's company, not mine. But at least let me get you some lemonade and cookies."

Without waiting for a reply, Eden darted back to the kitchen, where Hazel Farley had taken over the hostess duties. Grabbing a filled glass and a handful of cookies, she hurried outside again, half expecting to find Nicole gone. But Travis's daughter was still there, sitting with her knees drawn up to her chest. Trouble, Eden surmised as she held out her offering.

"Thanks." Nicole accepted the lemonade and wolfed down a cookie as Eden eased herself into a sitting position on the edge of the porch.

"Does your father know you're here?" she asked cautiously.

"No. But even if he did, he wouldn't care. My dad is the meanest man in the entire universe! Do you know what he did?"

Eden sighed, thinking this was the very last thing she needed today. "All right, tell me about it."

"He grounded me for two whole weeks! Two whole weeks on that boring old ranch, with no friends and nothing to do! I might as well be in jail living on bread and water! I might as well be dead!"

Eden bit back the temptation to lecture the girl. "So what did you do to make him so angry?" she asked gently.

"Nothing! I just wrecked his rusty old truck, that's all!"

"Wrecked his truck! Nicole—"

"Hey, I told him I was sorry. But no, that wasn't enough. He had to make sure I really suffered. He cares more about that beat-up old truck than he does about me!"

"So, you're supposed to be grounded, and your father doesn't know you're here." It was time to extricate herself, Eden realized. The last thing she needed was to be caught in a power struggle between Travis and this willful fourteen-year-old hellion.

"Oh, it's cool," Nicole said. "I told him I was going for a little walk. I just didn't say how far." Downing the last of her lemonade, she uncurled her legs and stretched them on the grass in front of her. Only then did Eden notice the awful condition of her feet.

Where the thin sandal straps had rubbed, Nicole's flesh was blistered raw. Dirt and stickers clung to the damp wounds, which were already starting to fester.

Eden swallowed hard as she stood up. "We've got to do something about those feet, Nicole. Come on upstairs. There's some hydrogen peroxide and antibiotic salve in the bathroom."

"Are you going to call my dad?" Nicole's eyes were as beseeching as a baby seal's.

"Somebody's got to call him. He'll be worried sick abou you. Come on." Eden held out her hand and pulled Nicol up, none too gently, considering her condition. Nicol limped beside her into the entryway.

"Eden, before we start on my feet, could I please use you phone? It's for a long-distance call, but don't worry—I'l make it collect. It won't cost you anything."

Eden paused at the foot of the stairs. "Do you mind tell ing me who you want to call?"

"My mom. I'm going to ask her to change my plane ticke so I can go home right away. I don't belong here. I belong in California."

The memory jabbed Eden like a dagger point—Travis a the airport, so eager to see his daughter, so elated about th summer ahead. Suddenly she was heartsick for him. "Ni cole, your father—"

"My dad won't care! The old grouch will be happy t have me gone."

"You're wrong." Eden steered her limping charge up the stairs. "I don't know your father very well, but I know how much he cares for you. I know how much he wants yo here."

"No, *you're* wrong, Eden. It's his sweet little girl Daddy wants. Not me. So, can I use your phone?"

"The answer to that question is no, young lady." Eden plopped Nicole down on the fuzzy blue toilet lid and be gan, very gently, to unbuckle her sandals. "I'm not getting pulled into the crossfire of a war between you and your fa ther."

"Nobody understands me!" Tears welled in Nicole's eyes and began to trickle down her cheeks. Eden steeled hersel against the pathetic sight. For all she knew, the little ma nipulator could turn them on and off like a faucet.

"Here comes the hydrogen peroxide," she announced, uncapping the brown plastic bottle. "It'll fizz, but i shouldn't sting much."

"That's okay. I'm tougher than I look." Nicole scrunched her face against the ordeal. "I've got something to confess to you, Eden."

"What?" Eden poured the disinfectant liberally on Nicole's blisters, catching the excess with a towel.

"On the way home from the airport, I— Oh, shi—*ouch!* I told you a lie."

"Oh?" Eden began smearing on the antibiotic salve.

"I told you my dad was still in love with my mom. The truth is, he can't stand her. And she can't stand him, either."

"I don't think your parents' relationship is any of my business, Nicole."

"Yes, it is. Isn't that why you told my dad you wouldn't go out with him?"

Eden lowered her face to hide the telltale surge of red. "My reasons for that are none of *your* business!" she insisted firmly.

"Oh, come on, Eden. My dad really likes you, no kidding! You should've seen how bummed he was when he hung up the phone—and I can tell you like him, too! What's the—"

"Enough, already!" Eden scooped up Nicole's sandals, which the girl would not be able to wear again until her blisters healed. "Come on downstairs and we'll find you something nourishing to eat. Then, Miss Nicole Conroy, you have a choice. Either you can call your father and tell him where you are or I'll call him for you."

"You can call him." Nicole huddled on the toilet lid, looking small and sad. "Eden, did you ever smoke?"

Eden paused in the doorway. "For a few months, in college. I thought it would make me look sophisticated, but it didn't. It only made me cough. After a while I got sick of the way my hair and clothes stank, so I quit. Any more questions?"

"Did your mom ever know about it?"

"Nope. So now it's our secret. Just yours and mine." Eden gave Nicole's shirt a playful tug, determined to avoid any more interrogation. "Enough stalling. Come along now, and let's see what's good in the kitchen."

Travis was hunched under the truck hood, reattaching a radiator hose, when he heard the phone from the house. For the first couple of rings he let it go, thinking Nicole would pick it up. Then he remembered her saying something about taking a walk around the ranch.

Blast it, how long ago had that been? An hour? Two?

Dropping his monkey wrench, he sprinted across the yard, took the front steps two at a time and caught the receiver in the middle of the sixth ring.

"Hello."

"Travis, this is Eden."

The no-nonsense tone of her voice was like the rasp of steel on raw silk—like Lauren Bacall inviting Bogart to whistle. But he had written the lady off, Travis reminded himself. This was no time for his hormones to shift into hyperdrive.

"Travis?"

"Uh-huh. What's up?" He tried to sound casual but it didn't fly. There was nothing casual about his reaction to Miss Eden Harper. It would be nice if she'd changed her mind about dinner, but judging from her brusque manner, he'd be smart not to bet the ranch on it.

"Are you, by chance, missing a daughter?" she asked archly.

"Nicole?" His mind flew backward to the girl's all-too-innocent announcement. "Oh, blast. What the devil has she done now? Don't tell me she's with you!"

"Right now, she's sitting at the kitchen table stuffing down her second helping of turkey noodle surprise."

Travis swore under his breath. "Did she tell you she was grounded? Let me talk to her!"

"In a second. What I was really hoping was that you could come and pick her up. Her feet are in no condition to walk home."

"Her feet?"

"They're blistered raw from her sandals. How soon will you be coming to get her?"

The cold formality in her voice irritated him like a burr. "For what it's worth, the truck isn't in any better shape than Nicole's feet," he growled. "I've got it torn apart replacing the radiator and the grille. Unless you want me to show up at your door on horseback."

"Throw in a suit of shining armor and you're on!"

Caught off guard, Travis teetered perilously between annoyance and amusement. "Today, you'd have to settle for head-to-toe grease," he muttered. "What kind of bribery would induce you to give Nicole a ride?"

"It's not a question of bribery, Travis. I just brought my mother home and we've got a house full of people. Maybe..." She hesitated, and in that small silence, Travis suddenly realized how desperately he wanted to see her again. "Maybe later, when things calm down," she said, "if you don't mind waiting."

"Fine. Maybe it'll give *me* a chance to calm down, too." Travis slumped against the table, noticing for the first time that he'd smeared black greasy fingerprints all over the phone. "How about staying for supper?" he heard himself asking. "I make a pretty decent stir-fry."

She froze on the line. "I don't—"

"Hey, this isn't a formal invitation. If you show up, you're welcome, that's all I meant." What was wrong with him? He sounded as awkward as a high-school sophomore asking for his first prom date! Next he'd be falling all over himself begging her to come!

"I—what—hang on a minute." Her words became muffled, as if her fingers were covering the mouthpiece of the phone while she spoke with someone else. Then she came back on the line, a note of hesitation in her voice.

"Uh, Travis, my mother says she and Rob would welcome some time alone this evening, so if you really want me as a dinner guest . . ."

"Great. Happy to have you." His pulse accelerated into high gear. "How does seven sound, providing you can put up with Nicole that long?"

"Fine. It's no trouble at all."

Travis took a deep breath, struggling to collect his wits. "Tell Nicole this little escapade will cost her an extra twenty-four hours."

"She's right here. Would you rather tell her yourself?"

Travis took time for a long raw breath. He knew his daughter was out of control, but chewing her out over the phone would only make things worse. Nicole needed something else. For the life of him, he did not know what it was, but somehow, somewhere, he knew he would have to find an answer.

"It can wait," he muttered. "Tell her to have her story straight by the time she gets home. And, Eden . . ."

"Yes?" The word was as soft as a breath and warm with the hint of promise.

"Thanks," he said.

It was dusk by the time Eden pulled the Buick through the open gate of the ranch. A single star gleamed above the mountains. Nighthawks swooped through the clear evening air, their white-barred wings flashing in the headlights. Except for the dismantled pickup and a couple of dogs, the yard was empty; but lights blazed through the windows of the two-story log ranch house with its broad covered porch.

Eden's heart broke into nervous flutters as she switched off the ignition. As a silly young girl, she had pedaled past the Conroy ranch more times than she could count, but tonight was the first time she had ever set foot inside the gate, let alone the house.

Nicole made no move to unbuckle her seat belt. "I don't want to go inside. What if he yells at me?"

"He could yell even louder if you don't get out of the car," Eden declared firmly. "Besides, he promised to make stir-fry. Come on—and don't forget your shoes."

As Nicole found her sandals, crawled out of the car and hobbled barefoot across the grass, Eden kept up her cheerful patter. Sooner or later she would probably regret taking Travis up on his supper invitation, but since her mother had nudged her into it, she had little choice.

"Don't hurry back for my sake, dear," Madge had chirped with an all-too-angelic smile. "Take as long as you like. Rob will take good care of me until you get home."

Even now, remembering, Eden groaned under her breath. Her mother's misguided matchmaking was already beginning to chafe. During her hospital stay and the drive home, the dear lady had found at least a dozen excuses to bring up Travis's name, and now even Nicole had jumped on the bandwagon. But none of it was going to work, Eden resolved. The very last thing she needed in her well-ordered life was to get involved with a small-town Don Juan like Travis Conroy!

"Hey, that stir-fry smells good!" Nicole sniffed hungrily. "I'm starved!"

"Starved? Then you must have a hollow leg. You've been eating all afternoon." Eden herself had been too busy to nibble. Her stomach was empty except for a flock of dizzy butterflies that refused to settle down. Seconds from now she would be seeing Travis again. No matter what happened, she vowed, she would not allow herself to be charmed, dazzled or intimidated by the man. She would eat her supper and make polite conversation. Then she would excuse herself, drive home and never look back.

Nicole reached ahead to open the door, then dropped behind her. Eden tensed as light spilled across the porch. Her pulse leapt as she crossed the darkened living room and stepped into the spacious country kitchen. Her eyes caught the gleam of varnished log walls, the cheery warmth of hand-braided rugs and red-checked café curtains...

And Travis.

He was standing next to an old-fashioned electric range, stirring something in a huge cast-iron skillet. "Hi," he said, glancing up as if Eden walked into his kitchen every day of the week. "This'll be done in a few minutes."

"It smells...heavenly." Her voice emerged as a nervous squeak.

"Thanks." Travis paused to give the mixture a liberal dash of soy sauce. He was wearing clean Levi's and a fresh denim shirt, its open collar a soft faded indigo against his golden skin. His dark hair curled wetly behind his ears. He had taken the time to shave and shower before supper, Eden realized.

"Can I do anything to help?" she asked, suppressing a ludicrous urge to reach out with a fingertip and stroke the crisp damp curls at the back of his neck.

"No, that's all right. It's almost ready. Besides, you're a guest. Here..."

He turned away from the stove long enough to pull a stout wooden chair away from the table. His bare forearm brushed against Eden's hair as she sat down, touching off sensations that rippled through her like the joyous sputter of a Fourth of July sparkler.

No, this was not a good idea. She should have made up some excuse, left Nicole in the front yard and driven away while she had the chance.

Struggling to collect her thoughts, she gazed across the table at the carefully laid place settings—the white stoneware plates on the hunter green tablecloth, the polished glasses, the folded cloth napkins, the small vase of wildflowers flanked by antique pewter salt and pepper shakers—

"Wow, cool!" Nicole had just walked into the kitchen. "Who are we entertaining tonight—Princess Di?"

"No, just my two favorite ladies." Travis's flip answer could not hide an undertone of strain. "Go on and wash up, Nicole. You and I can talk later."

"Right." She flashed out of the kitchen, clearly grateful for the reprieve. Seconds later Eden heard her limping footsteps overhead, followed by the sound of running water.

"So, tell me what happened." Travis had switched off the stove and was leaning against the edge of the countertop, his arms folded, his face troubled.

"She just showed up. I came outside and there she was, sitting on the lawn. She was pleasant enough—"

"Did she tell you she'd been forbidden to leave the ranch?"

"She said you'd grounded her for wrecking the truck." Eden could feel herself being pulled into the conflict. She fought to keep it from happening. "Travis, I'm hardly in a position to—"

"Damn!" His clenched fist glanced off the kitchen counter. "Eden, I'm at my wits' end. Nicole's all I've got. I'd do anything to make her happy here, but every single thing I try goes belly-up. We used to have such good times together, and now—"

"Travis, I don't—"

"What did she say to you?" His voice was gentle once more, but desperation still flickered in the darkness of his eyes. "Is there anything that would help? Anything I need to know?"

Eden's throat went dry as she remembered the collect call Nicole had asked to make. Should she tell Travis his daughter was scheming to go back to California? Could she say the words and watch him crumble?

"Nicole thinks you don't want her," she said softly. "She says all you want is to have your little girl back."

Travis's broad shoulders slumped. "All I want is for Nicole to be happy—and safe. Why is that so damn blasted hard for her to understand?"

"Fourteen isn't an easy age." Almost against her will, Eden's hand reached out and settled lightly on his wrist. His skin was warm, the muscles beneath taut and hard. "I've never raised a daughter of course, but I remember going through it myself. It's pretty rough when you're so anxious to be a woman, but don't quite know how to go about it." She paused with a self-conscious little laugh. "I wasn't much older than Nicole when I started writing you those ridiculous letters."

The flash of dark heat across his face told her she had said the wrong thing. She jerked her hand away as if her fingers had been burned. "I'm sorry. I didn't mean to—"

"No, it's all right." He turned back to the stove and began rearranging the stir-fry with a long fork. "You're speaking your mind, and I appreciate that. But you're only telling me what I already know—that things are bound to get worse. I can't afford to let things get worse, Eden. If they do, I'll lose her."

Something inside Eden plummeted like a lead sinker. She'd suspected all along that Travis wanted something from her. But she'd guessed it might have something to do with the class reunion. The idea that he needed her help with Nicole was a joke—no, worse than a joke. It was more like black comedy.

"Is that why you asked me out last week?" she demanded, fumbling in her jeans for her mother's car keys. "Is that why you invited me here tonight? To bail you out of this mess with your daughter?"

"Absolutely not."

"I don't believe you. And I don't like being used, even if it's for a good cause. Now, if you'll excuse me..." Eden had the keys in her hand and was halfway out of her seat when Nicole's limping footsteps on the stairway stopped her in midlunge. Travis shot her a warning glance as she shifted back into her chair and replaced the keys. It was too late to run. Until she could concoct a polite excuse to leave, she was stuck right here.

With a sigh of resignation, Eden settled back in her chair. She hadn't eaten since noon, and for whatever it was worth, Travis's stir-fry was making her mouth water.

Nicole padded into the kitchen, scrubbed, combed and subdued. Dressed in a loose-fitting denim jumper over a simple white T-shirt, she looked as innocent as a fawn, but Eden wasn't fooled. This child knew exactly where the buttons were, and she was pushing them.

"Hi, Daddy. Mmm, that smells yummy!" she warbled, bending over the skillet to sniff. "How did you learn to be such a great cook?"

"Anybody can cook if they read the recipe and do what it says," Travis muttered, keeping his guard up. "Try it yourself sometime."

"You mean that? You'd let me cook something? Like supper some night—for you and Eden?"

"Sit down. It's ready." He reached for a bowl on the counter and began dishing up the rice. Smiling like an angel, Nicole popped into the place next to Eden.

"How are your feet doing?" Eden asked.

Nicole grimaced adorably. "I won't be walking much for a few days, but I should be able to ride. Daddy and I are taking the horses out this Thursday. Maybe you could come with us."

Eden saw Travis blink in surprise.

"I've never been on a horse in my life!" she blurted, which was true. The farm kids and their friends had done plenty of riding, but as Edna Rae, she had never been included. Maybe if she had—

"Hey, there's nothing to it, is there, Daddy?" Nicole bounced forward, jiggling the silverware and the milk in the glasses. "I'll let you ride Tucker. He's old and slow, and he never bucks."

"That's not the problem," Eden insisted, determined to stop the nonsense once and for all. "Look, my mother just got out of the hospital. I need to stay home and take care of her."

Travis placed steaming bowls heaped with rice and stir-fried chicken with vegetables on the table. "Say the blessing, please, Nicole," he murmured, sliding into his chair.

Eden closed her eyes and clasped her hands under the table while Nicole mumbled a half-understood grace. She could not remember when she'd last been at a meal where someone had blessed the food. Even her mother had gotten out of the habit. But here it felt somehow familiar and comfortable.

Through the blur of her lashes, she cast a furtive glance at Travis across the table. The overhead lamp gleamed on his warm bronzed skin, accentuating the planes of his face, the sharp cheekbones and stubborn cleft chin. Eden remembered the old high-school assemblies and how she'd always tried to sit where her eyes could devour his profile or caress the curls at the back of his neck. Nothing had changed, she realized, except that he was older, more human, somehow, in his need for her help.

And she was as vulnerable as ever.

She remembered the Friday-afternoon dances at school, where the whole student body was herded into the gym. She remembered sitting wretchedly on the sidelines and watching the popular kids dance, aching as Travis glided by with Cheryl McKinley clasped in his arms. Their song was "Endless Love," she had overheard Cheryl telling another girl. Even now, Eden could not hear that recording without experiencing a jab of pain.

"You were peeking, Eden!" Nicole's impish voice jerked her back to the present. "I saw you—you were looking at my dad!"

"That's enough, Nicole." Travis's cheeks blazed under his tan. "Here, Eden, help yourself to some supper." He pushed the two bowls in her direction. Eden spooned rice and stir-fry onto her plate, her throat so constricted that she feared she might not be able to eat.

"Come riding with us Thursday, Eden," Nicole wheedled, picking up the conversation like a dropped ball of yarn. "There are plenty of nice ladies who'd stay with your mother if you asked—"

"I said that's enough, Nicole." Travis's tone carried an edge. "We invited Eden here to enjoy a meal with us, not to be harangued. Besides, she's going to think I put you up to it."

"Did you?" Eden shot him a narrowed glance.

Travis shook his head. "Scout's honor. But as long as we're on the subject, you *are* welcome to come, if you can manage to—"

"I can't," Eden insisted, crumbling a little under the pressure. "Don't ask me to explain again. I just . . . can't."

Travis cocked one black eyebrow. "In that case, let's eat. My masterpiece is getting cold."

Eden nibbled the stir-fry. It was delicious, the meat tender, the vegetables crisp and succulent, the sauce—

"Mmm! Daddy, this is orgasmic!" Nicole piped up.

Travis blanched. Eden surprised herself by giggling, and suddenly, miraculously, the tension in the room seemed to ease. They finished the meal in pleasant conversation. Nicole was polite. Travis was jovial, and even Eden did not trip over her tongue more than once or twice.

Dessert was store-bought vanilla ice cream with hot fudge sauce. When it was finished and the dishes carried to the sink, Nicole announced that she'd prepared a surprise.

"Both of you go into the living room," she ordered with a mysterious grin. "Sit down on the couch. I'll be right back."

Eden shot Travis a cautious glance. He was smiling broadly. "Relax," he whispered. "I know what she's up to. You're in for a treat."

Eden sank onto the edge of the massive leather sofa while Travis switched on a table lamp. The room was spacious and masculine, with varnished log walls, Navajo rugs on the floor, crowded bookshelves and a tall fieldstone fireplace. The only object on the mantel was a silver-framed photo of Travis's parents.

"I can see the work you've put into this house," she said softly. "Work and love. It's beautiful."

"Thanks." He settled back on the sofa, not quite touching her. "I did most of it myself a little at a time—stripped away the old plaster to expose the logs, hauled stones from the canyon to re-face the brick fireplace, enlarged the front window." He shook his head. "Building a new house would've been less work. But the old place meant so much to me I wanted to preserve it."

"Do your brothers and sisters make it back here often?"

"Not anymore." In the silence that followed, Eden sensed the loneliness of a man raised in a big noisy family. "They've got their lives," he said. "My life is here, on this ranch."

She might have encouraged him to say more, but at that moment, Nicole pattered into the room holding a thin silver flute in her hands. Perching on a stool, she raised the lovely instrument to her lips and blew a note so pure it made Eden quiver. Seeing her reaction, Nicole wobbled her black eyebrows—so like Travis's—in a roguish little half smile. Then she began to play in earnest.

Mozart. Ravel. Faure. Gershwin. All without sheet music. *She plays the flute like an angel,* Travis had boasted at the airport. Eden had dismissed the comment as fatherly ride. Now she realized what an understatement he had made. Nicole was more than talented. She had a remarkable gift.

Glancing at Travis, she saw how his face had softened in the lamplight. She saw the unguarded love in his dark eyes as he watched his daughter perform.

I can't afford to let things get worse. If they do, I'll lose her.

His words echoed in Eden's mind, and for the first time, she understood their urgency. But what could she possibly do to help? What did she know about handling a fourteen-year-old girl, especially a girl as bright, pretty and headstrong as Nicole?

No, even if she could help, she would be a fool to get involved. There were too many pitfalls, too many emotional traps. Travis meant well, but he was desperate enough to use her, and she couldn't let that happen. Run—that would be the smart thing to do. Run while she still had the chance.

Nicole had finished playing. Clearly pleased with herself, she lowered the flute to her lap. Eden joined Travis in an enthusiastic round of applause. "That was wonderful," she said, meaning it.

"I'm . . . a little out of practice."

"And out of breath." Travis gave her shoulders a heartfelt hug. "Thanks for the concert, doll."

"It's been lovely, but I really need to be going. My mother will be wondering why I've been away so long." Eden probed her jeans for the car keys. It wasn't true what she'd said about her mother. Time seemed to stop when Madge and Rob were together. But she needed to leave now. She didn't belong here—not with this man, not on this ranch, not in this town.

"I'll walk you to your car," Travis said. "Nicole, if you'd start loading the dishwasher . . ."

"Sure. Thanks for the ride home, Eden."

"And thank you for the beautiful concert." Eden had found her key ring. She gave Nicole's arm an awkward little squeeze, then turned hastily to Travis. "It's all right. I can find my own way outside. You don't need to—"

"Come on." His voice was gritty. His strong fingers gripped her elbow with a force that steered her through the front door and out onto the porch.

"G'night!" Nicole's cheerful voice sang after them as the door closed, shutting off the light.

Eden was alone with Travis in the soft blue darkness.

Intending to say goodbye and flee, she turned around, only to find him closer than she'd realized. A nervous hiccup jerked her diaphragm as she gazed up into glittering dark eyes, inches from her own.

"Excuse me," she murmured, stepping away in sudden panic. Her foot missed the top step, and she would have tumbled backward if he hadn't caught her arms.

"Careful." A smile played like light on his face, deepening those devilish dimples of his. Oh, she knew exactly what he must be thinking—that she was still a romantic little fool who would play right into his hands.

"I'd better be going. My mother—" She hiccuped again.

"Your mother's with Rob. She'll be fine for a few more minutes." He moved to one side, allowing her room to get her footing. "As long as you're here, let me show you around. I'm proud of this place. I'd like you to see what I've done with it."

"It's dark," she protested idiotically.

"Come on. Look, the moon's almost full!"

He moved along behind her, the pressure of his hand guiding her down the front steps to the lawn as the two dogs trotted behind them. In the distance, the town lay like a jeweled pin against the black velvet mountains. The wind whispered across the flat, ruffling the fields of sweet green alfalfa.

Eden's heart was thumping like the hands of a crazed bongo player. If she had any sense, she would break loose and bolt for the car. The night was too beautiful, this man far too dangerous for her tender emotions.

Travis thought he needed her—but it wasn't so. He didn't need her. He didn't even like her. To him, she would always be shy, clumsy Edna Rae, who'd had an embarrassing crush on him for half her lifetime.

If she let him, he would use her, then walk away and not think twice about it. Her feelings wouldn't matter. Not to a man like Travis.

He was capable of destroying her.

Chapter Seven

Travis guided Eden across the yard, his fingertips barely touching the small of her back. As often as he dared, he cast covert glances at her stubborn profile, eyes lingering on her soft full lips and the way her hair caught the platinum gleam of the moon. Eden Harper was a woman fashioned for moonlight, he reflected. She was a woman made for kisses and tender words, a woman made for love—despite every indication that she didn't seem to know it.

Travis burned to tell her. But even as the words took shape, he knew that telling her would not be enough. Not for her and certainly not for him. What he wanted was to *show* her. He wanted to touch her, to taste her, to sweep her into his arms and kiss her until they were both damp and dizzy.

But that wouldn't be a smart idea, his instincts cautioned. Eden clearly didn't trust him. And something told Travis she trusted herself even less. Where this particular lady was concerned, he would be wise to keep his hands to himself and his impulses in check.

If he could.

"What came over your daughter tonight?" she asked with a strained laugh. "She seems to have sprouted wings and a halo."

"Draw your own conclusions. That's the best I can do." Travis watched the faraway lights of an airplane skim the horizon and wink slowly out of sight. He had never regretted staying in this little town, but sometimes he wondered how his life would have turned out if he'd left. Would it have made a difference with his marriage? With Nicole?

Was this new wild streak of his daughter's somehow his fault?

"At least you've discovered there's another side to Nicole," he said, pulling his attention back to Eden. "You had a part in bringing it out tonight. Thanks for being here."

Her waist stiffened against his hand. "Travis, I—"

"Look—a falling star!" He pointed at empty sky, lying through his teeth. Oh, he knew what Eden wanted to tell him. He knew she had no desire to get involved, with him *or* Nicole. But he wasn't ready to hear her say it, not yet, at least. He needed her fragrant softness beside him. He needed her voice and her touch. Something in him could not stand to watch her walk away.

"Come on," he said. "Let me show you my horses."

Travis had built the stable seven years ago. It was spacious and modern, with electric lights, running water and sixteen twelve-foot stalls for his prize quarter horses. There was a loft for hay and straw, and, off one end, a tack room with grooming and medical supplies, as well as a shed for the long sleek horse trailer.

Eden blinked as he switched on the lights. "This is...amazing," she said, her gaze sweeping the rows of immaculate stalls. "It's like something out of 'Dallas'!"

"You were expecting the O.K. Corral maybe?" Travis chuckled self-consciously, feeling like a kid on his first date. "I'm glad you're impressed. I wanted you to be. But when it comes to horses, some things never change. Keeping this place up takes a helluva lot of shoveling.''

She laughed—the tickly, raw-silk laugh he remembered from the airport, a laugh so low and lush it was almost caress. Travis found himself wondering what it would be like to hear that lovely laugh next to his ear in the intimate warmth of his parents' big brass bed. He imagined himself finding ways to bring out Eden's laughter, to pamper and cherish her every waking moment...

For an instant, he forgot to breathe.

What was the matter with him? He had found Eden attractive from the moment she walked out of the jetway, but he'd never planned on losing his head, let alone his heart. Now he felt as if he had just plunged off a tall cliff.

Travis's head reeled with implications—more than he could sort out now, with Eden's nearness singing a siren's song in his head. What he needed was time alone. Time to think. Time to talk some sense into himself. Otherwise, he was in for one rough emotional ride.

But that was easier said than done. Patience and restraint had never been his strong points. When he wanted something, he tended to go after it with all the stops out.

Mostly that worked to his advantage. The only trouble was, what he wanted this time was Edna Rae Harper.

She was hesitating, straining toward the door. Propelled by a sudden urgency, Travis seized her elbow. ''Stick around,'' he said, struggling to sound casual. ''I'll introduce you to the gang.''

Eden strolled along the row of stalls, trembling with the awareness of Travis's presence at her shoulder. His fingers guided the small of her back, their warm pressure igniting rocket flares from her ears to her toes. She breathed deeply, flooding her senses with the sweetness of fresh hay and the rich pungent aroma of horses. The old collie nudged her hand with its pointed nose, and she reached back to scratch its head. Travis was watching her. His dimples deepened bewitchingly as he smiled.

Oh, this was not a good idea. He was being far too attentive, and she knew it wasn't because he liked her. To get help with Nicole, the man would do anything—even cozy up to Edna Rae Harper.

She struggled to ignore his nearness, making polite comments as he showed her his precious quarter horses. They were splendid animals, to be sure, but the truth was, Eden had never felt comfortable around horses. They made her nervous, with their lunging bodies, their big yellow teeth and their bone-chilling snorts and whinnies.

As a three-year-old toddler, she had wandered into the street during a Fourth of July celebration. A high-strung parade horse had jumped and reared, knocking her over with a glancing blow from one front hoof. She had not been seriously hurt, but the terror of that moment had remained, frozen in the dark recesses of her mind.

And now it was beginning to melt.

"This is Jackknife." Travis paused outside the stall of a rangy buckskin. "He's a gelding—doesn't have the conformation for show or breeding, but he's as smart as a mule and as surefooted as a cat. Great mountain horse. I wouldn't take any amount of money for him."

Eden kept a safe distance. "You sound as if you're introducing me to your family," she murmured, forcing a smile.

Travis grinned. "I guess they are family—except maybe those four big colts on your left. They're Storm Cloud's babies. I'll be saddle-breaking them this summer, and then they'll be going to the big auction in Amarillo. Their price should keep the ranch running for the next year, so I can't let myself get too attached to them."

"And, uh, when do I get to meet Storm Cloud?" Eden braced herself for the inevitable.

"He's in that corner stall. Come on." Travis reached out and caught Eden's hand, his strong fingers interlacing with hers. Eden's legs had gone watery. She seemed to float along beside him, anchored only by his compelling grasp.

"Take a look. This boy's got a pedigree as long as your arm." Releasing her hand, he unlatched the door of the stall and opened it wide enough for her to see inside. The stallion, a silvery roan, raised his elegant head with a snort. Storm Cloud was not as large as Eden had expected, but even her untrained eye could sense the fire that smoldered in every muscle of his compact body. Her mind groped for something appropriate to say.

"He's like...a Greek statue," she whispered, terrified of startling the high-strung animal. "Is he fast?"

"Very. But I can't risk racing him. He's too valuable. Come on, I'll show you what I mean." Latching the door again, he guided her to the opposite corner of the stable where a soft-eyed bay mare, her belly huge with foal, shifted restlessly in an oversize stall.

"This is Chocolate," Travis said, the tenderness in his voice trickling through Eden like a warm current. "Last summer I drove all the way to Tennessee to buy her and bring her home. Her bloodline and Storm Cloud's..." He reached out and patted the mare's bulging side. "Let's just say I've got a lot of hope riding on this lady and her boyfriend over there."

Eden allowed him to lead her past the rest of the stalls, her polite facade masking a panic that swelled with each heartbeat. She was out of her depth here. With the horses. With Travis. She would not feel safe until she was back in the car, headed for home.

"And here's Tucker," Travis announced, pausing outside the last stall. "Tucker was a grand champion cutting horse in his prime. The old boy's getting pretty long in the tooth now, but I keep him around because he's such a gentle soul. Anyone can ride him. Anyone at all."

"Anyone?" Eden's heart lurched. "Even me? Is that what you're suggesting?"

"Even you. Any time you'd care to try."

Eden peered cautiously into the stall, expecting to see some doddering nag. But Tucker was as big and scary as the other horses. When he saw her, he nickered, shook his coppery hide and butted his massive head toward her. Startled, Eden stumbled backward, almost falling into Travis's arms.

"I...I'm sorry," she stammered, fighting for balance. "I haven't been around horses much. I'm just not used to them."

Travis chuckled in disbelief, his hands thrusting her forward again. "Don't be nervous. Tucker's as friendly as a big old pup. See, he wants you to stroke him."

Stroke him? Eden stared up at the huge head, wanting to pull away and run. Travis would laugh at her, she reminded herself. Anything, even touching a horse, would be preferable to that.

Holding her breath, she stretched out a hand and ran a trembling fingertip down the glossy flat of Tucker's cheek. The hair was coarse and sleek, its texture guiding her touch downward to the velvety skin of his muzzle.

"Why...he's so soft," she whispered, her fingers exploring in wonder. "I've never—"

Whulff! Tucker snorted loudly, showering Eden's palm with moisture. She jumped like a rabbit, lost her footing and again tumbled backward against Travis's chest.

"Easy." His throaty laugh stirred the hair at her temple. His big hands braced her ribs, his fingers warm and hard through her thin cotton shirt. "It's all right. Old Tucker's just talking to you."

"Well, I certainly can't credit him with a dry wit!" she snapped, wiping her hand on the seat of her jeans. "I'm sorry, Travis, but I don't have much of a way with animals, especially horses."

"Oh, come on, you can make friends with him. Anybody can." He moved in close behind her, then eased her gently forward, his touch sending her pulse into cart-wheels. "That's it. Take a deep breath and try it again."

"I . . ." Eden hesitated, panic muddying in her mind. No, she couldn't go on with this charade! Between Travis and the horse, she couldn't even think straight. She twisted away from him, struggling for self-possession.

"No, I don't want to try again," she declared. "I've never liked horses, and this one seems to feel the same way about me. It's time I was getting home."

"Is it just the horse, Eden?"

His question riveted her. She turned sharply to find him standing at her shoulder, his rugged face cast into shadows by the stark overhead light.

"I don't know what you're talking about," she murmured, turning away to hide the crimson that flooded her cheeks.

"Yes, you do." His hand flashed out to cup her jaw, lifting her face, forcing her to gaze directly into his eyes. "Listen to me, Eden Harper. You're a beautiful intelligent lady, and, damn it, I *like* you! I'd welcome the chance to get better acquainted, maybe have a little fun while we're at it. But every time I try, you skitter off like a spooked trout! Blast it, I won't hurt you any more than that old horse will! Don't you know that?"

His eyes shot bullets of frustration. Eden's heart hammered her rib cage. Maybe she'd wished too hard for Travis in the old days. Maybe those wishes were coming back now to haunt her.

"What's wrong?" he asked more gently. "Is it that I'm just not your type? Have things changed that much since high school?"

"Don't!" She jerked away from him, her face blazing. "This *isn't* high school! I'm not Edna Rae anymore! I'm not the girl who wrote those stupid letters! I've grown up, and I'm too smart to be taken in by your flattery!"

Something flickered across his face, almost as if she'd cut im, but he swiftly recovered. "Flattery, is it?" His eyes linted. "Sorry, lady, I may plead guilty to a few sins, but sincerity isn't one of them. You've got to come up with a etter excuse than that."

"My mother says you could have any woman in the ounty. So why me, Travis? What is it you want?" She hesated, then plunged on without waiting for an answer. "It's Nicole, isn't it? You think she's taken to me. You think I can omehow influence her. Well, I'm sorry, but you're barking up the wrong tree. I don't know anything about teenage girls, and what's more—"

"What's more, you talk too much, Eden Harper."

His arm hooked her waist, crushing her against his hard lat belly. Eden's breath caught in a muffled gasp. Her heart uivered, then broke into a rampaging gallop as his seeking mpatient mouth covered her own.

Travis's kiss began harshly, almost roughly, but the conact of their lips and bodies sent shock waves of sweetness hrough them both. Eden's resistance melted against his eat. She softened in his arms, her lips swelling to meet the rgency of his kiss. How many times had she imagined his—Travis's hands molding her body to his, his mouth aressing her, nibbling her, tasting her.

Eden's breathing grew ragged as his hands explored her ack, fingertips skimming her hips and the sensitive oundary of her breast beneath her arm. Yes, she wanted im to touch her there, to touch her everywhere she'd reamed of him touching her. She wanted—

A tiny nervous hiccup shattered her thoughts, wrenching er back to reality. She was Edna Rae Harper, she reminded herself, the girl nobody wanted. Travis was only aking advantage of the moment. In the end he would laugh t her. The whole town would laugh at her.

"No!" She'd gone rigid against him. His arms released er, dropping to his sides. Eden could not read the expression on his face as she staggered backward, her unsteady legs scarcely able to support her. "No," she whispered again. "I can't do this, Travis. I can't play your game."

"Nobody said it was a game." His voice was husky, his lips damp and swollen from kissing her. "Eden, you can't just walk away from this."

"No, I can't." She fought for strength, her senses still reeling. "I'm not capable of walking away from you. I'm going to have to *run!*"

Her vision blurred as she spun away from him and raced out of the stable. Travis did not follow her, but she could feel his gaze on her, raw and painful, as she plunged into the darkness and sprinted across the yard.

The green Buick was unlocked. She flung herself inside and slammed the door. Her eyes, reflected in the rearview mirror, were large, luminous and strangely beautiful. Her heart was pounding like a jackhammer.

Travis's kiss and the memories of her own fevered response blazed through her body. Even the thought of it left her weak and dizzy, and she knew she could not lose control again. She could not allow herself to feel what she'd felt in Travis's arms. It was too dangerous, too frightening.

She had to get out of here.

Eden jammed the key into the ignition and cranked the starter. Nothing—unless you counted the sickening buzz that told her there was no juice coming from the battery. Muttering under her breath, she tried again, with the same result. Then, just to be sure, she switched on the dash lights.

Nothing.

The car was not going to start.

Quivering with frustration, she slumped over the wheel. She could see light from the open front door, where Nicole had come out onto the porch. She could see Travis walking out of the stable.

Oh, damn! Damn, damn, damn, damn!

Mustering her dignity, Eden rolled down the window and waited for Travis to cross the yard. He took his time, moving down the driveway as if he was out for an evening stroll.

"Something wrong?" he asked, pausing next to the car.

"Battery." She could not look at him.

"Pop your hood latch, and I'll see what I can find. Got a flashlight?" His manner was a stranger's, detached and impersonal, as if that soul-searing kiss had never happened.

"Here." She fished the light out of the glove compartment.

"Hop out. I'll need you to hold it." He raised the hood and propped it open. "Hang on, and I'll get my tools out of the pickup. With luck, it'll just be dirty terminals."

Climbing out of the car, she switched on the flashlight. Nicole had come limping over from the porch. Eden was grateful for her presence. They exchanged comments about the car as Travis retrieved his toolbox and opened it on the ground.

"Hopefully this won't be too hard to repair," he muttered, selecting a hefty screwdriver. "Otherwise, we'll have to send you home on Tucker."

"Just fix it. Please." Eden focused the flashlight beam on the top of the battery. One terminal connection was crusted with seepage. She would have the battery replaced tomorrow, Eden vowed. But first she needed to get home.

"Tucker's a big old love, isn't he, Eden?" Nicole's curly head bobbed into the light. "I know you could ride him if you tried. And I could ride Moonfire on Thursday, couldn't I, Daddy? I'm old enough to handle her now. Please say yes—and you, too, Eden. We could have so much fun!"

Travis scowled as he loosened the clamps on the battery terminals. "Yes to your riding Moonfire, I suppose. But I don't know about Eden. She and Tucker didn't exactly hit it off. The old boy took to Eden all right. But the attraction didn't seem to be mutual." He flashed Eden a sharp glance.

"If you want to know the truth, I think she was plain scare of him."

"Scared? Of Tucker?" Nicole stared at Eden in disbe lief. "Why, Tucker wouldn't step on a bug if he knew it wa there!"

Eden felt the color rising in her face. "I wasn't scared, she sputtered. "I was just being cautious around a strang animal."

"Uh-huh." Travis used the screwdriver blade to scrape th corrosion off the battery clamp. "And I'll bet money you' be scared to ride him, too."

Eden fought the urge to strangle the man. "That's not so I can't go riding because I need to take care of my mothe and that's the truth!"

"Your mother's got more friends than any woman in th town. Any one of them would be happy to keep her con pany for a few hours. All you have to do is ask." Trav glanced up from reattaching the clamp. "You're too cov ardly to climb on Tucker's back, Eden Harper. I'm so su of it that I'm willing to make you a little wager. Name yo stakes. What do you want from me if I'm wrong?"

Eden glowered at him. She knew she was being rai roaded, but there was no graceful way out—except, mayb to make the stakes so high Travis would call off the bet.

"That old pickup of yours," she said, thinking fast. "I you're wrong about me and I ride Tucker, you have to trac it in on a new truck—with air-conditioning!"

"Cool move, Eden!" Nicole clapped her hands as Ede congratulated herself on the scheme. She couldn't care le whether Travis replaced his truck, so even if he hung toug and she forfeited the bet, there was no way she could lose

One thing was certain. She had no intention of climbin on that spit-blowing monster of a horse.

His eyes narrowed to penetrating slits. "Let me get th straight," he said. "You ride Tucker—not just hop on an off, but stay on him for at least a mile—and I have to buy a new truck. Right?"

"Right." Eden couldn't help feeling smug.

Travis hesitated, his thumb working the screwdriver as he tightened the clamp. "All right, it's a deal," he said, wiping a grease-smudged hand on his jeans. "Here, shake on it."

Eden shook his hand, her fingers trembling in the cocoon of his big warm palm. Travis cocked one eyebrow as he released her. His eyes had taken on a crafty glint that suddenly made her uneasy.

"Now for your part of the wager," he said.

"My part?"

"You didn't expect this bet to be one-sided, did you?"

"Riding the horse is my side," Eden declared stubbornly.

"That's the action, not the stakes." He gave the clamp a final tightening twist and dropped the screwdriver back into his toolbox. "I put up the truck. You have to put up something of equal value." He pretended to be in deep thought while Eden fought the urge to lambaste his beautifully cleft chin.

"I've got it," he declared with a grin. "You lose the bet or try to weasel out, Miss Eden Harper, and you'll go to the class reunion. As my date."

Eden's heart plummeted to her socks as her predicament sank home. Much as she feared riding a horse, the thought of walking into the crowded high-school gym was infinitely worse.

She shot Travis a murderous glance. "I'll take Tucker over you any day," she muttered. "All right, what time do you want me here on Thursday?"

"As early as you can get here, since we'll want to beat the hot sun. See how things work out with your mother." Travis's eyes were blandly innocent as he lowered the hood of the

car. "It should start now, but I'd replace that battery if
were you. Jump in and try it."

Grateful for the break, Eden climbed into the car, turned
the key and pumped the gas. The roar of the Buick's engine
was music to her ears. "Thanks!" she shouted as she
switched on the headlights, shifted into reverse and backed
down the drive. Travis flashed her a maddening wink as he
bent to gather up his tools. Nicole was waving.

"See you Thursday!" she yelled. "And don't worry
Eden, you're going to love it!"

You're going to love it! Oh, yeah, Harper. *You're going
to love it!*

Eden repeated Nicole's words like a mantra as she pulled
the Buick through the open gate of the ranch Thursday
morning. The moment of truth had arrived.

She slipped out of the car and closed the door quietly behind her. The house looked quiet. Maybe Travis and Nicole
had overslept. Maybe they'd forgotten about today. Maybe
she could just slither back into the car and . . .

But there would be no escape. Travis was already out
side. As Eden came around the house, she could see him
near the stable, bending low to adjust Jackknife's saddle
girth. Two other horses were tied to the corral fence. One of
them was Tucker.

"Hi!" Travis had seen her. He straightened and waved
"You're right on time. Nicole should be out in a minute or
two."

"You're depressingly cheerful this morning." Eden forced
herself to smile as she tottered toward him on legs that
seemed to be made of wet spaghetti. The other night's kiss
blazed like fox fire through her senses. There was no way she
could look at him or hear his voice without remembering.

His eyes took in her trim jeans, white linen shirt and nar
row leather concho belt. "I'm just glad to see you. I was
afraid you might not show up."

"And have you drag me to that reunion? Not a chance."
:den's laugh came out sounding more like a nervous
himper. She stared at the big bay horse, her courage wa-
ering. "Travis," she murmured, "I don't know whether
iis is such a good idea."

"The horse? Or you and me?"

"Stop it. There *is* no you and me."

A shadow flickered across his face, then vanished. "All
ght, one thing at a time. What's wrong with old Tucker
ere?"

"Nothing—I mean, it's not Tucker. It's me. I had a bad
xperience with a horse when I was little. I've been afraid of
iem ever since."

"Horses and men. I think I'm beginning to understand
ou, Eden Harper."

"Don't bet on it." She stared at the ground, grateful that
licole would soon be joining them. Travis had a way of
ying waste to her defenses, leaving her vulnerable and ex-
osed.

"Look at me, Eden." His thumb lifted her chin. His dark-
shed eyes studied her face, as if they were measuring the
irit inside. "Fear is only as strong as you give it permis-
on to be. You can let it run your life, or you can turn your
ack on it, even if it's only a little at a time."

"Oh, stop preaching!" She twisted away from him, but
is strong fingers captured her wrist in a grip that refused to
t her go.

"Trust me," he insisted. "You don't have to be afraid."

Eden went rigid as he drew her gently toward Tucker. This
me there was no stall to protect her from flying hooves.
here was nothing but clear morning air between her and a
iousand pounds of snorting stamping fury.

Tucker was munching a wisp of hay. He opened one
rowsy eye as she edged toward him. His long black tail
hisked a stray fly off his rump. From where Eden stood,
e looked as big as an elephant.

"Talk to him," Travis coached. "Let him know you wa to be friends."

"You're asking me to lie?" She inched closer, Trav backing up her courage with a tight clasp on her arm. H had accused her of cowardice, Eden reminded herself. Pri demanded she prove him wrong.

"Hi, Tucker," she quavered. "Are you ready to take n for a nice ride, you old sweetheart?"

"That's it," Travis whispered, his breath tickling her ha "Now try patting him." When she hesitated, he guided h hand along the glossy curve of the big gelding's nec Tucker's hide was like warm satin. A shiver of pleasu passed under Eden's palm as she stroked him. "Oh . . ." s breathed. "Travis, he's really lovely—like a nice big dog!

"What did I tell you?" His chin brushed the tip of h ear, sending an echoing tingle through every nerve in h body. "As long as you're feeling brave, let's try somethi else."

Stepping away from her, he fished in his shirt pocket a came up with two lumps of sugar. "Give him these, a Tucker will be your friend for life."

"You want me to *feed* him?"

"Trust me." Pressing the sugar into her hand, he guid Eden's wrist, gently this time. "Now, open your hand fl Don't try to cup it. That's it."

Tucker had scented the sugar. His big head jerked u Eden's heart stopped. Her knees wobbled as the huge ve vety lips brushed her palm. Then the sugar was gone.

"See, you did it!" Travis gave her an enthusiastic h from behind. His arms lingered, then softened. His mou brushed a light kiss along her temple. An exquisite lit tremor, like the slow unfolding of a violet, rippled throu Eden's body. She closed her eyes, knowing she had to bre away. Travis Conroy was poison to a woman like her. The could be no future in any kind of relationship with hi Sooner or later, he would—

"Hi, Eden!" Nicole's voice sang out on the morning air. Hot-faced, Eden spun away from Travis as his daughter came bounding across the yard. "Hey, you showed up! Daddy was betting me you wouldn't!"

"Oh?" Eden shot Travis a withering glance. "Your daddy has a lot to learn," she declared archly. "Especially about me."

Travis grinned. "You talk big, lady. Now let's see you put your money where your mouth is and climb up on that horse!"

"Right. Just give me a second." Eden took a shaky breath, plumbing the depths of her courage. She'd managed to pat Tucker and even feed him, but climbing onto his back was something else again. The saddle looked twenty feet off the ground, and the worst thing was, Tucker was underneath it.

"Need any help?" Travis looked so smug Eden could have punched him.

"I've seen plenty of Western movies!" she huffed with a lot more bravado than she felt. "I know how it's done!"

Travis watched, half-amused, as she edged close and put a shaky hand on the saddle horn. "Well, ma'am, you'd better start by goin' around the horse," he drawled. "Even ol' Tucker here's a mite fussy 'bout not lettin' folks up on his starboard side."

Eden reddened beneath her sunscreen. "I knew that," she muttered, stalking briskly around to Tucker's left flank. In truth, she *hadn't* known it, but she would die before admitting her ignorance to Travis. The big show-off was having too much fun as it was.

Much too much fun. And at her expense.

Suddenly Eden was furious with herself. She'd been acting like a little ninny, allowing Travis to lead her around by the hand. What was the matter with her? A woman who'd survived on her own in New York City could certainly muster the courage to climb onto a horse!

Propelled by her anger, she shoved her left foot into the stirrup and swung her whole body upward. Her heart played leapfrog as she worked her right leg over the horse and shifted her rump into the saddle.

Travis and Nicole broke into spontaneous applause a Eden blinked in amazement. She was sitting the horse, facing the right direction, with both feet in the stirrups. Sh forced herself to laugh. "See," she said, with a little toss o her hair, "nothing to it."

It was a good act, but her confidence was mostly show Her skin broke out in cold sweat as Travis untied the rein and reached up to place them in her hands. An image of th rearing parade horse flashed through her mind. Her stom ach clenched in silent fear.

"Hey, there." Travis's eyes were warm in the mornin sunlight, his hand warm, too, on her trembling knee "You'll do fine," he whispered. "Just stay close to me."

Eden nodded mutely, her heart flip-flopping like a hooke trout. But this time it wasn't the horse. It was the mai looking up at her. It was the sunlight dancing off the clear chiseled planes of his face. It was the lingering pressure o his palm through the fabric of her jeans. Suddenly, gettin bucked off a horse was the least of Eden's worries. The ho little shimmers that coursed through her body told her sh was in deep trouble, getting deeper by the second.

"I'm okay," she muttered, tearing her gaze away from him. "Let's go."

"Right." Travis vaulted lithely onto the buckskin. He sa a horse with the grace of an old-time Western hero, Ede reflected, head proud, posture easy, as if he'd been born t the saddle.

Good grief, has my brain gone back to high school? Nex thing I know, I'll be comparing his features to a Rodi bronze!

Nicole had swung onto the third horse, a silver-coate filly with the unmistakable stamp of Storm Cloud's blood

e. She grinned at Eden, clearly pleased with herself for
ogressing beyond sedate old Tucker. Then with a high-
irited whoop, she jabbed the filly's flanks and rocketed
ward the front gate.

"None of that!" Travis shouted after his daughter. "You
ld her back or we call off this jaunt right now, and you
n't ride her again!"

His threat sparked a flicker of hope in Eden's heart. She
sn't ready, in any sense, for this ride. Even if she could
y on the horse, she knew she couldn't hold her own
ainst Travis. She was no match for his movie-star looks
d easy charm. Another hour with this man, and she would
blithering like a high-school freshman.

Her spirits sank as Nicole reined in the mare and trotted
r back to the fence. "Sorry, Daddy," she murmured
eetly. "I was just feeling her out. Can we start now?"

"Let's go." Travis nudged Jackknife to a walk. Eden fol-
wed his example, her hands white-knuckled on the reins
Tucker snorted and broke into an ambling jog.

Travis eased his horse alongside her. "Relax," he whis-
red. "Put your weight into the stirrups—that way you
n't bounce so much. Just watch me, and do what I do.
u'll be fine."

Eden thrust out her chin and fixed her face in a deter-
ined smile. "I *will* be fine," she declared. "And while
're on the subject, Travis, what color is your new truck
ing to be?"

He flashed her a heart-stopping grin. "Black," he said.
Big, shiny and black as the devil's own heart!"

Chapter Eight

The sun crept above the eastern peaks, its light warming the brushy flats from silver to pale gold. The lyric song of a meadowlark quivered on the morning air, punctuated by a squawk from a magpie on a juniper limb. The dogs romped along through the sage, dashing ahead, then trotting back as if to say, *Come on, can't you hurry?*

Travis loved the peace of mornings on horseback, but he felt no peace today. His mind was a jumble of clashing emotions, and the harder he tried to sort matters out, the more confused they became.

First there was Eden—bright beautiful Eden, who stirred longings so sweet and deep they made his whole body ache. Even now, the memory of her in his arms set his pulse to galloping like a hormone-crazed eighteen-year-old's. But that was only the surface of the problem. Hormones he could deal with if he had to. But what if the attraction was more?

What if he was falling in love with her?

He stole a sidelong glance as she rode beside him, chatting with Nicole. She wasn't doing too badly on old Tucker. In fact, he was damned proud of her. Eden had been so genuinely afraid of the horse. Yet she had pulled herself together and climbed on his back. How many women would have done that? In six years of marriage, he'd never been able to talk Diane onto a horse. Diane would have told him to take his horse and—

Damn!

Travis's gut clenched as the crux of his dilemma sank home. After his miserable experience with Diane, he'd sworn that the next woman in his life would be a small-town girl, one who would be content to grow old with him on the ranch, sharing his life and raising his babies. For nine years he'd searched among the local ladies, hoping something would click. It never had.

Until now.

For all his cautious and wise intentions, he had fallen for another city woman.

"Look! A hawk!" Nicole pointed to a circling figure in the sky. Travis followed the direction of her gaze, thinking his daughter had been much too angelic these past few days—much too obedient and much too cheerful. She had helped out in the stable and kitchen, made her bed every morning and even practiced her flute. It would be nice if he could credit the transformation solely to Eden, but Travis knew better. Something was up.

Why, for example, had she been so eager to go on this ride? Their last horseback outing had been a fiasco, with Nicole griping and pouting most of the way. This morning she'd gotten up at dawn and was prancing along on the mare, looking as pert as a spring chickadee. She was beginning to make him nervous.

"Would you let me come to New York and visit you sometime?" she was asking Eden. "I wouldn't be any trouble, I promise. You'd hardly know I was around."

"Maybe when—you're—older." Eden's words jerked out between sharp breaths as Tucker lurched through a shallow wash. "But—even then, it would have to be—up to your parents."

"You don't just invite yourself to visit someone, Nicole," Travis lectured her gently. "You wait for an invitation."

"Oh, Daddy, you're so old-fashioned!" Nicole tossed her curls, then froze in midmotion as a dark moving shape appeared over the horizon. It was a rider. Male. Young. Galloping closer.

Travis's spirits plummeted as Nicole whooped and began to wave. He'd been right about the little schemer. She'd engineered this whole outing, and now he knew why.

The rider, who was slim, sandy-haired and looked about sixteen, reined in his horse with a friendly grin. Travis recognized him now. He was Jess Erickson's youngest, a decent kid from a big farm family across the flat.

What the hell. At least it wasn't Turk with the cool Harley tattoo.

"Daddy, Eden, this is Matt," Nicole announced with an air of fawn-eyed innocence. "It's okay if he rides with us, isn't it?"

"Sure." Travis fought the urge to grind his teeth. His daughter was growing up, he reminded himself. And at least this time, the little minx would be chaperoned.

Matt swung his horse alongside Nicole and the two began talking. Before Travis knew it, the youngsters had pulled ahead by a good twenty yards, leaving him with Eden.

Which, now that he thought of it, wasn't all bad.

He edged the buckskin closer, his boot almost brushing her leg. "You're doing fine," he said. "I'm right proud of you, Eden Harper."

"Well, I hope you'll be equally proud of your shiny, new, black, air-conditioned truck." She kept her eyes forward, allowing Travis to study the way her hair fluttered back from her face. She was beautiful this morning, with the sunlight like fresh cream on her fair skin. Maybe he ought to tell her so.

Or maybe he ought to keep his fool mouth shut.

"I could take a few lessons from your daughter," she said with a self-conscious laugh. "I swear, that little imp must give off pheromones."

"Uh-huh." Travis scowled at the two young riders, who were gaining distance by the minute. "But the kid's got me running scared. I'd gladly pay some wicked witch for a spell to make her homely and backward for the next few years— say, until she has a chance to finish college."

"Homely and backward." Eden let the horse pick its way around a big clump of rabbitbrush. "Like me, you mean?"

Her question hit him like a dash of ice water. "I was joking," he said. "And you just took a cheap shot at one of my favorite ladies."

"It's nothing to joke about." Her fingers tangled nervously in Tucker's black mane. "I had what seemed like a lifetime of being Edna Rae the nerd, and believe me, there was nothing funny about it. I wouldn't wish my high-school experience on my worst enemy."

Travis shook his head in mild surprise. Back in high school, he had never paid Edna Rae much attention, but somehow, in his insensitive young mind, he'd assumed she'd chosen to be what she was and was more or less happy that way. "Come on," he said, humoring her, "how bad could it have been? At least you were a great student. You were always on the honor roll."

"And you think that was enough?" The pain of memory flickered in Eden's heart-stopping eyes. "You don't know how much it hurt, always being an outsider, never fitting in, never belonging. Someone like you—you can't even imagine it."

A meadowlark's song echoed across the flats. Travis squinted at the sunlit peaks, taking his time, struggling to make sense of what Eden was telling him. "Is that what you think?" His voice was rasp-edged, cutting into her awareness. "You think I've lived some kind of charmed life? That I've never known what it feels like to be left out?"

"How could you?" She clasped her hands on the saddle horn, leaving the horse to find its own way through the brush. "You were always the golden boy. You had everything. You still do."

Travis muttered his disbelief. "Look at me, Eden." His fingers flashed out and clasped her wrist, the contact between them so electric that as she turned on him, eyes wide and bewildered, he was forced to let go. "Look at who I really am. This isn't high school anymore—you said so yourself. It may not show, but in my own way, I've been through as much rejection as you have."

Eden yanked a yellow bloom off a clump of rabbitbrush and twisted it between her fingers. "All right, tell me," she said. "Convince me how rough you've had it, Travis."

Travis exhaled, ignoring her none-too-subtle jab. "You called me the golden boy. That's a joke. My family was dirt poor, and I worked my hands to blisters on that ranch," he said. "I know you didn't grow up rich, either. Nobody did in this little town, so it didn't make much difference. But in college—"

"You did have an athletic scholarship," she reminded him so archly that Travis could not be sure if she was truly skeptical or just egging him on.

"Oh, the scholarship helped," he said, taking her comment at face value. "But between classes and basketball practice, there was no way I could hold down a job. I didn't even have a car that first year."

"Join the club." She tossed the sprig of rabbitbrush at his head. "At Utah State, I bussed tables in the dorm cafeteria, bought my clothes in thrift shops and rode a secondhand bike to class. At least you had the glory of being on a college basketball team."

"Glory! You've got to be kidding!" Travis nudged his horse to a trot. Eden followed his example, bouncing hard in the saddle. The stoic expression on her face told him how much it hurt, but she kept her complaints to herself.

Only when Nicole and young Matt were well in sight again did he ease the buckskin to a walk and take up the thread of the conversation. "I didn't get ten minutes of playing time in my whole college career," he said. "I spent most of the games sitting on the bench."

Her eyes flashed genuine disbelief. "But you were so good! You were All State—"

"I'm six foot two. Even for a guard, that's not big enough to cut it in college ball. Not when you're going up against seven-foot centers. I'd been a star in high school, but in college, I felt like a nineteen-year-old has-been. And that was about the time I met Diane."

Eden glanced away, her eyes fixed on the space between Tucker's ears. In the tick of silence that followed, Travis mentally bit his tongue. He should have known better than to bring his ex-wife into the conversation. But then, it wasn't the first dumb thing he'd done since Miss Eden Harper had walked into his life.

"If Diane is anything like Nicole, she must have been a real dazzler in college," Eden ventured.

"She was. Sorority girl. Homecoming queen attendant. Drove a Corvette. She could've had any guy on campus, but she went after me. Lord, it happened so fast. I was still in shock when she told me she was pregnant, and we got married two weeks later."

"That doesn't exactly sound like rejection to me," Eden commented dryly.

"Don't count me out till I'm finished." Travis's sardonic response hid wounds that stung like raw rope burns. "Diane's parents treated me like an outcast, especially when I insisted on supporting her myself. I quit the team and took a night job driving a forklift. For a girl who'd grown up with the best of everything, it wasn't much of a life. If it hadn't been for the baby, we'd probably have split up long before we did.''

He paused for breath, thinking that if he wanted to charm a lady, this wasn't the way. Why did he always end up baring his soul when he was with Eden? Why did he feel this need for her to know everything about his life?

It was time to change the subject, he reasoned—but no, she was waiting for him to go on, her soft pink lips parted expectantly. Fighting the urge to chuck all caution, grab her out of the saddle and kiss her silly, Travis cleared his throat and continued the story.

''After graduation, Diane was all for our going back to California. Her dad offered me an assistant director's job in one of his funeral homes, at a salary so high I knew it was a gift. He meant well, but it was plain as mud he didn't think I was capable of providing for his daughter without charity.''

Travis's mood darkened as he recalled the emotional scene, his own proud anger, Diane's tearful outrage. ''I told the good man what he could do with his offer. Then I got a teaching job in Monroe and took my family home to the ranch.'' He paused to guide the horse around a twisted cedar stump. ''When I look back now, I realize I was selfish and arrogant, demanding that Diane be happy on my terms. I should've known even then how things would turn out.''

''My mother told me about how your wife left,'' Eden said. ''She heard the whole story from her hairdresser. I guess I'm not the only one who gets gossiped about in this town.'' Her hands tightened nervously on the reins, even though Tucker did not even flinch as two jackrabbits bounded across the path and vanished into the brush. ''Have you ever been sorry you came back here?''

''Not really. When I look around the ranch and see what I've built, I know I made the right decision. It's mine. It's where I belong and what I want to do. Even so, at the end of every summer, when I take Nicole back to the airport and put her on the plane, the same old doubts come back to chew on me, and I wonder if, somehow, I could have made a difference...."

Travis gazed across the flat, toward morning-shadowed foothills velvety with sage, juniper and rabbitbrush, thinking how much he loved this wild clean country and how he would have hated the crowds, freeways and big smoggy cities of Southern California.

He glanced at the woman at his side, wondering if there was a chance she could ever feel as he did. Eden had fled small-town life for the big city. But her roots, like his, went deep into the rocky gray soil of this little valley. If there was any chance she could be happy here, he had to know. Otherwise, the only wise choice would be to walk away before they both got hurt.

"How about you?" he ventured, feeling as if he'd just stepped onto a patch of quicksand. "Do you see yourself spending the rest of your life in New York?"

Eden gazed into the distance. Travis waited, counting eternities before she replied. "I...don't know. Last winter, along with my wedding plans, I dreamed up this lovely bucolic future in a country house with a red swing set in the yard and the school bus stopping at the front gate. I imagined Chet taking the train to Manhattan and me editing out of a home office, doing some magazine articles on the side, maybe even a children's book. But that dream went up in smoke when I sent Chet's ring back. Now that it's over, all I can think of is survival."

Travis felt his pulse leap. Be cautious, he warned himself. Don't take it too fast.

"Haven't you ever wondered what might have happened if you'd come back home after college, instead of going to New York?" he asked.

"No. No, absolutely not." She shook her head so vigorously her hair swung outward, scattering sunbeams. "I *know* what would have happened here—nothing! My life in Manhattan is no party, but at least it got me away from Edna Rae. She never bothers me there. It's only when I'm in Utah that she comes back to haunt me.''

Travis hid his dismay with the quirk of an eyebrow. "That's funny. I don't see her anywhere.''

"Then look harder, Travis. Edna Rae is right in front of you. Shy and awkward and scared to death.''

"Scared? Of me?'' Travis reined the buckskin to a snorting halt. His free hand grabbed Tucker's bridle, forcing the big bay to stop, also. "Look at me, Eden. The last time we were together, I held you in my arms and kissed you. And you kissed me back. I don't know what was going through your head at the time, but judging from your reaction, it sure as blazes wasn't fear.''

"You're making a fool of me,'' she said, jerking at the reins in an effort to pull away from him. "If I thought you felt anything real, it might be different. But to you, all I am is an interesting challenge.''

"Eden, if you'd listen—''

"No, *you* listen! I know you think you're attracted to me. But it isn't *me* you're seeing, Travis. It's *Eden!* It's the bleached hair and the New York clothes and the contact lenses! Take away the trappings, and there's nobody here but nerdy little Edna Rae, who wrote you those idiot letters and who still dies of humiliation every time she looks at you!''

She swung the reins sharply to one side. As the bridle tore loose from Travis's grip, she dug the toes of her tennis shoes hard into the big gelding's ribs. Even for placid old Tucker, the surprise was too much. With a sharp whinny, he veered off the trail and exploded like a rocket.

Eden flew straight up, feet jerking clear of the stirrups. An instant later she was sprawled in a patch of green tumbleweed, and Tucker was bucking his way across the flat like a rodeo bronc.

Sick with fear, Travis dropped the buckskin's reins and vaulted out of the saddle. Eden had taken one hell of a fall. She could have broken bones or spinal injuries or worse. She could...

Relief washed him in cold sweat as she sat up and pressed her hands to her face.

"Damn it, are you all right?" Travis hadn't meant the words to sound harsh, but they came out that way.

"I...I think so." She flexed her hands and feet, stretching tentatively. "Nothing seems to be broken. But I'm going to have some interesting...bruises." Her face tightened in pain as she struggled to stand up.

"Here." He caught her under the arms, his throat raw with emotion. Where his hand gripped her ribs, he could feel her whole body shaking. Still dizzy with relief, he swung her onto her feet, then lashed out in sudden anger.

"Of all the crazy things to do—spooking a horse like that! You could've broken your fool neck or been dragged halfway to Arizona, or..."

The words died in his throat as he saw the tears welling in her eyes, spilling over her thick golden eyelashes. "I'm sorry," she whispered. "I didn't realize how hard I'd kicked him or what he'd do. It would've served me right if I *had* broken my fool neck."

"Blast it, will you stop apologizing for yourself?" Travis was being unreasonable now, he realized. But this woman was so damned precious, and she had scared him so badly. If anything had happened to her—

"Stop apologizing, you say!" A spark of anger flared in Eden's eyes. "Don't you see, that's the whole problem, Travis? Back in New York, I'm competent, professional Eden Harper. But with you, I'm just one big walking apology! Edna Rae strikes again."

Travis certainly hadn't planned on kissing her. But somehow it seemed like the most natural thing in the world that his arms had softened around her, that his lips were nibbling the salty tears from her cheeks, her nose, her glorious rose-petal mouth. Eden strained against him, then, as her resistance crumbled, curled against his chest with a little whimper. Her arms pulled him down to her. Her lips molded to his warmth, mouth opening in dark moist welcome to the sensual probings of his tongue as he kissed her again and again, wild with the feel and scent and taste of her.

"This...is crazy, Travis," she murmured against his moving lips.

"Crazy, but nice." His tongue grazed the softness of her eyelids, then returned to plunder the satin honey of her mouth.

"No..." She struggled halfheartedly. "We can't do this now."

"Why not?"

"The horse...Nicole..."

The mention of his daughter jerked Travis back to reality as nothing else could have done. He remembered his last sight of her, prancing into the sage on the spirited mare, the Erickson kid hovering around her like a moonstruck gander.

"Fatherly duty calls," he murmured, releasing Eden with a reluctant sigh. "Hang on, and I'll round up Tucker. Will you be able to ride him?"

"It beats walking back to the ranch." She managed a tremulous grin as he turned toward the buckskin. "Travis?"

He glanced back over his shoulder.

"You and I need to talk," she said.

"Uh-huh," he agreed, sensing what she had in mind and thinking there were things he'd much rather do than discuss why their relationship was a bad idea. "Let's hold that thought till we get some time, okay? For now, we've got some heavy-duty chaperoning to do."

He found Tucker cropping grass beyond a clump of junipers. The big bay had settled down enough to be led back to where Eden was waiting and to stand still while she mounted. Travis felt a flicker of pride as she declined his help and thrust her foot unhesitatingly into the stirrup. He would have told her what a plucky lady she was, but something told him that any praise from him would only make her uncomfortable.

"You had a pretty good scare," he commented as she eased into the saddle. "Will you be all right?"

"Certainly!" She flashed him a too-bright smile and patted the horse's shoulder. "Tucker and I will get along fine. We're learning to respect each other, aren't we, old boy? Now, come on, let's catch up with Nicole and Matt."

She urged the big gelding to a trot, bouncing gamely in the saddle. Travis sensed the unease in her, but he had no way of knowing whether it was triggered by the horse or by the chemistry that had flared like tinder when he'd held her in his arms. He only knew that he wasn't ready to give up on her, city woman or not. What he felt with Eden was too good, too rich with promise, to let her get away without a fight.

Ahead on a low ridge, he could see the two youngsters resting their mounts, the dogs beside them. Nicole waved as she spotted him, and Travis knew he would have no more chances to be alone with Eden that morning, which was probably just as well. They could both use some cooling-down time.

He hadn't quite figured Eden out. For that matter, he probably never would—that was part of what made her so delicious. But their conversation had given him some insights and some ideas. If Eden's aversion to small-town life was as strong as Diane's, he would be smart to give up now and walk away with what remained of his pride. But if the problem was Edna Rae, the situation called for some creative thinking.

She had been right about one thing. They did need to talk. But not just yet, Travis resolved. First he wanted some time, and the chance to lay some very important groundwork.

* * *

Eden's muscles screamed as she stepped over the edge of the tub and lowered herself gingerly into the steaming bubbles. After four hours on horseback, she felt as if every joint in her body had been through the Spanish Inquisition. No part of her, she swore, would ever be the same again.

She closed her eyes as the blessed heat seeped into her limbs. It was one o'clock in the afternoon, and the temperature outside was pushing ninety, but she didn't care. A hot bath was exactly what she needed. When she finished soaking, she promised herself, she would pull on her sloppy old sweat suit and spend the rest of the afternoon at the kitchen table, editing the manuscripts she'd brought from New York. Maybe a few hours of honest concentration would help take her mind off Travis.

But there was nothing to distract her now. As Eden relaxed in the scented bubbles, the morning's events rolled through her mind like scenes from an old B-grade cowboy movie. The headstrong heroine. The unruly horse. The fall. The celluloid-melting kiss that went on and on....

Oh, it was all so *corny!* And the worst part was her own behavior. She'd become so caught up in the melodrama that she'd lost all common sense.

With a self-deprecating scowl, Eden sank deeper into the gardenia-scented bubbles. It was time to be realistic, she lectured herself. Once and for all, it was time to thrust her adolescent fantasies aside and grow up.

Very sound advice. The only trouble was, those fantasies had a disturbing way of coming true.

A dreamy smile flitted across her face as she pictured Travis on horseback, so dark and erect, so proud. Her eyelids drifted closed. Her tongue traced a tingling line along the curve of her lower lip as she remembered his ravenous kisses—kisses that had left her breathless and hungry. If they'd had more time alone—yes, at night, under a black velvet sky, glittering with a million stars, and maybe a cashmere blanket to spread on the glistening sand...

Good grief, I'm doing it again! Fantasizing like a moon-eyed fifteen-year-old!

The hot bath might be helping her sore muscles, but it wasn't doing a thing for her libido. Disgusted with herself, Eden yanked the rubber plug out of the drain, clambered out of the tub and wrapped herself in her old chenille robe. Maybe her mother needed company. Or maybe that last piece of Faye Osborne's key lime pie was still in the fridge. Anything to take her mind off Travis.

She made her way stiffly down the stairs to find her mother lying on the sofa, legs covered by a lacy crocheted afghan. Her periwinkle robe brought out the blue in her eyes, the pink in her cheeks and the soft silver in her hair. Rob's diamond sparkled on her finger.

"You look radiant," Eden said, meaning it. "Love must be great medicine."

"You could use a little yourself," Madge said pointedly. "How was the ride?"

"Well, at least I conquered the horse. I'll never be afraid of riding again. But everything has its...price." Eden winced as she lowered herself into a corner of the sofa at her mother's feet. She didn't feel ready to talk about the near accident or Travis's soul-shattering kiss. She needed time first to sort things out in her own mind.

"Well, what about you and— Oh, I just remembered!" Madge exclaimed, blessedly changing the subject. "Rob picked up the mail for us this morning. There are two letters for you on the kitchen table." Her sharp blue eyes narrowed. "They're, uh, both from New York."

Eden stiffened, struck by the dark note in her mother's voice. Hobbling into the kitchen, she found the two envelopes next to a pot of African violets. One of them bore the Parnell Publishing imprint in the upper left-hand corner.

The other... Her stomach went leaden as she recognized Chet's precise accountant's penmanship.

"Well?" Madge called out from the sofa.

"Mother, you're shameless!" Eden pattered back into the living room with the two letters. "Just to make you suffer, I'm going to open the one from Parnell first."

Sitting down again, she ripped off the end of the envelope and shook out its contents—her monthly paycheck in a smaller sealed envelope, along with a note from Denise Schwartz, one of the other editors. To mollify her mother, Eden read the note aloud:

> Just wanted to say goodbye while I had the chance. Mark's accepted a transfer, and we're moving to Vermont next week. I'm going to miss you, but here's the nice part. I'll still be working for Parnell. They're allowing me to set up a home office with my own computer, modem and fax machine. I'll even be able to phone-conference in on the meetings. In terms of efficiency, it'll be almost like working in New York. Isn't technology great? I only wish—

"You could do that, too!" Madge interrupted.

"Move to Vermont? I hardly think so."

"Oh, stop playing dumb." She jabbed Eden's hip with a slippered toe. "You could set up a home office and work anywhere. Even here!"

Eden groaned, remembering her morning conversation with Travis. Things were falling into place too neatly, too fast. "Mother, why would I want to live anywhere except New York?" she demanded.

"Well—" Madge fiddled with the afghan's long fringe "—things happen. Have you ever thought about it?"

Eden sighed. "When you were in the hospital, I did think about moving to Salt Lake to be closer to you. But the circumstances are different now. You'll have Rob. You won't need me."

"Oh, sweetheart, don't be silly. I'll always need you." Madge strained forward, wincing as she reached to squeeze her daughter's arm. "Go on now, stop stalling and open the other letter."

Eden's fingers shook as she freed the single page from its stiff formal envelope. All the humiliation, all the injured pride washed over her again as she unfolded the paper. Maybe Chet was marrying someone else and wanted her to know. Maybe he thought that she owed him money, or that she'd kept one of his PDQ Bach tapes, or hung on to his spare apartment key.

Bracing herself for the kind of verbal drubbing that only Chet could deliver, Eden began to read—silently this time. She could not trust herself to speak his words aloud.

She read the first paragraph, then the second and third, her reaction swinging between cold outrage and the urge to laugh like a maniac.

"What?" Madge was as pop-eyed as a little girl at the circus. "What does he have to say?"

"He . . . says he wants me back."

"You're joking."

"Read it yourself." Dazed, Eden sank back into the sofa cushions, the letter open on her lap. "In his own words, he's reconsidered his decision to cancel the wedding. When I get back to New York, he wants to get together over dinner and talk about our future. *Our future!* Can you imagine it?"

"Are you all right, dear?" Madge had made no move to pick up the letter.

Eden nodded weakly. "I guess so. I just don't know whether to laugh or cry, that's all. Chet hurt me so much. And now, reading his letter and realizing what a conceited, self-important—"

"Priggish. Wasn't that my word for him?"

"Priggish." Eden swallowed hard. "Oh, I feel like such an imbecile!" She crumpled the letter and hurled it to the carpet. "Do you want to know the worst part? When I read the letter, for an instant, just a heartbeat, I actually thought about giving him another chance."

"You'd really do that?"

"No. Of course not. How could I?"

"But you still want children, don't you?" Madge asked gently. "Before the wedding, you told me how much you wanted a family."

"Yes, I know I did." Eden remembered her fantasies about the country house and the red swing set. More short-sightedness on her part. Chet had wanted to stay in Manhattan, and he'd reacted with a nervous twitch every time she mentioned babies. Maybe that was part of the reason he'd come down with a case of cold feet.

"I'm trying very hard *not* to want children anymore," she said. "It's foolish to keep wishing for something you'll probably never have."

"Eden—"

"No, listen, Mom. I'm almost thirty years old, and I've got to accept the fact that time's running out. But hey, at least I've got a good mind and a promising career. My life could certainly be worse."

"Sweetheart, you don't have to settle for—"

"Of course—" Eden faked a calculating smile "—I could always take Chet up on his offer."

"You wouldn't!" Madge looked truly horrified.

"I could spend the rest of my life pruning his bonzai and ironing his sheets, and in return, he could keep my checkbook balanced to the penny."

"Stop it! Don't scare me like that!" Madge had begun to giggle.

"I could have the kids shrink-wrapped so they wouldn't leave sticky handprints on his glass-topped Lalique coffee table, and send them off to boarding school so they wouldn't upset their father's nightly reading of the *Wall Street Journal*. I could—"

"Eden, stop it!" Tears of agonized laughter trickled down Madge's flushed cheeks. "You're hurting my stitches..."

But it was no use. Eden was laughing, too, her body shaking with raw-edged hilarity. The pain was still there. So was the anger. But the thought of Chet's letter—the bald-faced ludicrousness of his expectation—washed through her in hysterical waves again and again, until she collapsed, exhausted, in her mother's arms.

Morning came much too soon. Eden yawned, turned over to glance at her bedside clock and realized it was almost seven-thirty. She had stayed up until late last night red-lining an especially troublesome chapter of Parnell's new middle-school history text. It had been nearly one when she'd given up and staggered upstairs to bed, and she was still sleepy. Another hour of drowsy oblivion would be delicious. But her mother was probably lying awake in bed needing her help. It was time to get up.

Flinging back the covers, she swung her legs to the floor. *Oof!* Her sore muscles had stiffened during the night. Eden lurched painfully across the room, grabbed her robe and limped down the hall. Her mother was still asleep, her face relaxed in a dreamy smile.

Fighting the temptation to crawl back into bed, Eden headed for the shower. The stinging water warmed her limbs and washed the cobwebs from her brain. She would spend the day in safe sane editing, she resolved. No more crazy jaunts on horseback. No more cowboy fantasies. And especially no more fantasizing about Travis. Yesterday he had literally swept her off her feet. Today it was time to be sensible. All chemistry aside, Travis's world was here in this remote little town. Her own world was anyplace *but* here. Why complicate both their lives by getting involved?

She stepped out of the shower to the sound of her mother's radio. Flinging on her robe, she hurried down the hallway to find Madge sitting up in bed. "I think I can manage the bathroom on my own this morning," she said. "Why don't you go downstairs and rustle us up some breakfast?"

"Coming right up!" In her room, Eden pulled on her jeans and a faded black T-shirt. Ten minutes later, she was climbing the stairs again with a tray that held oatmeal, toast, orange juice and a fresh rose from the bush that grew outside the kitchen door. She found Madge washed, combed and back in bed.

"Here you are," she said. "I—"

The brisk honk of a horn just outside cut her off in midsentence. "Noisy neighbors," she muttered, setting the tray on the bed and moving to close the open window. "How can they expect anybody to..."

Eden's jaw sagged as she looked between the curtains.

Below in the driveway was a brand-new pickup truck—big, shiny and as black as the devil's heart.

At the steering wheel, grinning like a Cheshire cat, sat Travis.

Chapter Nine

Nicole was standing on the front porch, one finger poised to ring the doorbell. She waved as she spotted Eden leaning out the upstairs window. "Hey, come on down!" she shouted. "My dad wants to take you for a ride!"

Eden shook her head, determined to make the day turn out exactly as she'd planned. "I'm sorry, but my mother needs—"

"Hey, it's cool. I can stay here and keep your mother company while you're gone. Come on, Eden! It's such a kickin' truck! You've got to ride in it!"

"That's very nice of you, Nicole, but I really don't think—"

"Oh, go on, dear," Madge urged from the bed. "Get out and enjoy yourself. I'll be fine with the child here."

Eden's resolve began to collapse under the double assault. Maybe it would be a good thing for her to go. The short drive would give her a chance to lay things on the line with Travis. Their relationship had already gone too far. Once and for all, it was time to put an end to this lunacy.

"Hang on," she said. "I'll be down in a minute." Dashing back to the bathroom, she scrubbed her teeth and ran a comb through her hair. As an afterthought, she added a dash of lipstick, blush and eyeliner. She wasn't out to impress Travis, but she did have her pride.

"Don't worry, I'll take good care of your mom," Nicole reassured her as they passed in the front hall. "Have a great ride!"

Travis had climbed out of the truck and was waiting for her in the driveway. The grin on his face eclipsed the glow of morning sunlight on the peaks.

"So, what do you think?" he asked, looking as proud as a little boy with his first bicycle.

"It's, uh, a very nice toy." Eden stared at the massive vehicle, overpowered by its size and sleek shiny newness. "So take me for a quick spin around the block. I've got a mountain of editing to plow through today."

"Climb aboard." Cupping her elbow, he steered her around to the passenger side of the truck. Travis's nearness touched off a surge of memories—his arms clasping her close, his hungry seeking mouth and her own explosive response to his kiss. Eden's face flamed as his hand lingered an instant longer than necessary, and she realized he was remembering, too.

"Up you go." He released her to open the door to the cab, which looked impossibly high. Her overstretched muscles screamed as, feeling clumsy and ridiculous, she raised one leg, winced with pain and staggered backward.

"Need a boost, lady?" Travis's strong hands caught her waist, lifted her high and swung her into the seat. "Maybe I'll hang a stirrup on this side of the truck. Then getting in will be just like climbing onto old Tucker."

"Don't remind me," Eden muttered, reaching for the seat belt. The truck's interior was as posh as a luxury sedan, with rich leather upholstery, velvety carpeting and a dashboard that looked like the control panel of a 747. "You really wen first class," she commented as Travis swung into the driver's seat.

"I tend to go all out. Or haven't you noticed?" He shifted the truck into reverse and backed it down the driveway, its engine purring like a big black cat.

"Just a spin around the block," Eden cautioned. "I have a lot of work to do."

"Uh-huh." Travis eased around a corner and headed straight for the center of town.

"What are you doing?" Her heart lurched into a panic-stricken gallop as she realized what he was up to. "Travis, what are you thinking? Everybody will be looking at this truck! They'll see us together!"

"Uh-huh." He did not even slow down.

"You know what they'll say!"

"If they say anything at all, it'll be, 'There goes that lucky Travis Conroy with a brand-new pickup and a beautiful blond passenger.'"

"Stop this truck and let me out!"

"Can't hear you!" He had flipped on the radio. A wailing rendition of "Stand by Your Man" blared out of the expensive stereo speakers as he swung the truck around the corner, eased up on the gas and headed due south down Main Street.

Eden scrunched low in the seat. Then, realizing how ridiculous she must look, she sat up again and did her best to appear nonchalant.

Main Street was busy for such an early hour, with people bent on running their errands before the daytime heat set in. Travis slowed the truck to an infuriating crawl, grinning back at everyone who looked his way.

Eden cringed as she spotted LaVerne Filstrup, who worked at the bank with her mother and considered spreading local news part of her job description. She was standing in front of the post office with Wanda Randolph, the city librarian. Both of them waved enthusiastically as the truck paraded past them.

"Why are you doing this?" Eden wailed, slumping in her seat. "You know how I feel about being seen with you!"

"Uh-huh." Travis had turned off the radio. He raced the engine and waved at a man on a farm tractor. "That's the whole idea. You and I may be the talk of the town for a day or two, but after that we'll be old news. We'll be able to go anywhere in the county without raising eyebrows."

"You're crazy."

"Thank you." He shot her a devilish smile.

"Kidnapping is a federal offense."

"Sue me." He passed the church and kept on driving all the way to the south end of Main Street where the road swung east toward the canyon. Only then did Eden realize where he was taking her.

"Travis, I don't have time for this," she argued. "My mother—"

"Your mother is in perfectly good hands."

"Did you let Nicole in on this crazy plot?"

"Yup."

"And she went along with it?"

"Absolutely." Travis shifted into third as the truck roared uphill toward the mouth of the canyon. "Not that the little minx doesn't have her own agenda. Nicole's figured out that if her old man is occupied with his own pretty lady, he'll have less time to spend riding herd on *her*."

"So, that's why she was so anxious to have me come horseback riding with you."

"You've got it. Nicole ran into Matt the day she walked to your house. She knew I would never let her out alone while she was grounded, so with a little help from him she cooked up the entire scenario—even called him from the house before we left so his timing would be perfect. I weaseled the whole confession out of her last night."

"The little schemer!" Eden caught herself laughing. She rolled down the window of the truck to let in the fresh morning air. The wind was cool and sweet against her face.

"We had a pretty good talk," Travis said. "Nicole told me she'd tried to call her mother from your house and you wouldn't let her. Why didn't you tell me that?"

Eden's gaze followed the rocky foothills that flanked the mouth of the canyon. "I . . . guess I didn't have the heart. I kept hoping things would get better and you wouldn't have to know."

"She also told me she'd decided to quit smoking for good. It seems you'd told her it wasn't, uh, cool. I owe you big time, lady."

"I can't take any credit for that," Eden murmured, disturbed by the warmth in his voice. This conversation was getting out of hand, and she wasn't happy about it. "What about Matt?" she asked, hoping to steer things in a different direction. "Are you going to let her see him again?"

Travis sighed with fatherly resignation. "Matt's a pretty nice kid, so I guess I can afford to bend a little. No dating. She's too young for that. But we did agree that he could visit her at the ranch and come along on a few outings. They're already planning a trip to Fish Lake after the holiday. You're invited of course. In fact, that was one of her stipulations. No Eden, no Fish Lake."

"Travis—"

"She'd be awfully disappointed if you said no."

Eden slumped in her seat, realizing she'd been corralled, roped and hog-tied yet again. "All right. But it's got to be the last time, Travis. We can't go on seeing each other."

"And why not, since it's pretty obvious we both enjoy it?"

"You know why not." Eden stared out the window as the truck rumbled past towering rocks and bushy clumps of scrub oak. The paved road ended at a picnic area a couple of miles up the canyon, so this ride couldn't possibly last much longer. Sooner or later he would have to turn around and take her home.

"Suppose you tell me," Travis said. "Come on. I'm all ears."

Eden chewed at a hangnail as they passed into the narrows, where jutting cliffs loomed on both sides of them. Below the road, the creek rushed and sparkled over the rocks. "It's the town," she said. "And it's me. And it's you."

"You're not making sense."

"That's because you're not trying to understand. I could never be happy here. And you could never be happy anyplace else."

"Nobody said we had to make it permanent." Still going fast, he splashed through the shallow channel where the creek crossed the main road, then shifted down and spun the wheel sharply to the right. The tires spat gravel as the truck roared onto a steep unpaved side trail that climbed dizzyingly up the side of the canyon.

"What are you doing?" Eden gasped.

"Just checking out the truck. I want to see how she climbs. Hang on, city lady."

"Travis, this wasn't—in the—plan!" Eden's voice went up and down as the big vehicle lurched along the rutted road.

"Plan?" He glanced at her, one black eyebrow sliding upward. "What plan?"

"*My* plan! My plan for today! My plan for my whole life! I don't belong here—in this truck, in this town..."

"No one's forcing you to stay, Eden. But when something this good comes along, why not grab on to it and enjoy the ride for as long as it lasts?"

"You sound like my mother."

"Your mother's a very wise woman."

"But her advice never seems to work for me." Eden shook her head vehemently. "I can't seem to do things b

half measures, Travis. I just went through the breakup of
one relationship, and it isn't in me to go through that kind
of trauma again. The next one has to be for keeps. That's
why it—can't—be—you.''

"Look." Travis eased off on the gas pedal. The road had
emerged from the canyon into a glorious panorama of valley, mountains and sky. The air was diamond clear and rich
with the fragrance of earth and pine.

"I know it isn't Manhattan," he said, "but as long as
you're here, you might as well take it all in."

"Travis, I don't—"

"Be still and enjoy the ride." His voice was gentle, with
a husky edge that raked Eden's pulse. "That's what this
morning is all about."

The truck wound its way up the rutted dirt road, higher
and higher, purring through thick groves of pine and aspen, emerging again and again to vistas that took Eden's
breath away. She clung to the edge of the open window,
saying little. There were no words for how beautiful it was.

"You've never been up here before?" Travis asked.

She shook her head, awestruck by the grand sweep of sky
and the barren crests of the Tushar Mountains to the south.
"I've been in the canyon of course. Everybody has. But no
one's ever driven me up this road. I barely knew it was
here."

"Still mad at me?" he teased.

"That's a loaded question. Where are we going?"

"You'll see. It's not much farther."

The road leveled out and wound east across the top of the
high wooded plateau, then descended into a grassy bowl
where a small azure reservoir glistened like a mirror in the
morning sunlight.

"Here we are." Travis pulled the truck off the road, set
the brake and sprinted around to help Eden down from the
cab. She tensed, quivering with awareness as his big hard
hands gripped her waist and swung her to the ground. Her

heart flailed like a trapped moth as his warm gaze penetrated hers. He was too close, too real, too openly determined to win this conquest of her emotions.

She had never felt more vulnerable in her life.

Sensing her nervousness perhaps, he released her and strode back toward the tailgate of the pickup, which, by now, was spattered with mud. "Hungry?" he asked. "I brought along some breakfast."

Without waiting for her reply, he lifted a picnic hamper and a faded patchwork quilt from under a protecting tarpaulin. Eden glimpsed the edge of a white linen cloth poking from beneath the lid. "You really *did* plan this, didn't you?" she asked, trying to sound flippant, but falling short of it.

Travis's only answer was a mysterious wink before he turned away, whistling softly. Eden followed his long strides to a sheltered patch of grass, a stone's throw from the water's edge. Her stomach responded to the thought of food with an audible growl. Travis had snatched her away from the house without breakfast, and she was truly hungry.

"Do you always treat your prisoners this well?" she asked as he spread the quilt on a level spot and motioned for her to sit down.

"Only the ones I'd like to keep around for a while."

Eden's throat tightened. "Travis—"

"Relax. I brought you up here to enjoy yourself, not to threaten your virtue."

"Very funny." She settled onto a corner of the quilt, hands clasping her knees. The air was vibrant with the calls of bluejays and chickadees and the drumming echo of a woodpecker. Sunlight danced on the blue surface of the reservoir. Wild daisies, purple specks of lupine and clumps of feathery Indian paintbrush dotted the grassy meadow.

Relax.

If only she could.

Travis opened the picnic hamper and spread the linen tablecloth between them. "My mother's," he explained, his fingertips skimming the embroidered violets along its edge. "She was seventeen when she made it for her hope chest. Knowing her, I don't think she'd mind our using it this morning."

Eden's eyes widened as he reached into the hamper to produce starched linen napkins, bone-china plates, antique silver and a pair of exquisite little porcelain cups with matching saucers. Next came the food—luscious red strawberries and sliced cantaloupe, grapes like translucent jade, Camembert cheese on a little marble platter, flaky croissants, still warm in their insulated basket, accompanied by butter and orange marmalade.

"You *made* these?" she asked.

"With a little help from the Pillsbury Dough Boy." Travis's too-ready laugh carried an undertone of strain. Only then did Eden realize how anxious he had been to please her.

To please *her,* Edna Rae Harper, the zit queen of South Sevier High.

With a self-conscious flourish, he reached into a corner of the picnic hamper and produced the crowning touch—a single red rose in a crystal vase. His brown eyes were tender but guarded. "I, uh, know this isn't the Four Seasons, but..."

"Don't apologize." A burr of emotion pricked her throat. No man, not even Chet, had ever gone to much bother just for her—and for *breakfast,* of all things. The gesture was so splendid she had to fight back tears.

Travis was waiting. Eden knew he wanted her to say more, to let him know she appreciated what he'd done. She groped for the right words, something clever but not sarcastic. something sincere but not too emotionally revealing. something—

Her stomach spoke for her. The low resonant growl echoed like the rumble of an approaching thunderstorm.
Crimson-faced, she stared out at the water.

The dimples deepened at the corners of Travis's mouth as
he bit back a smile. "Well," he drawled, "I guess that says
it all. How about some coffee? Or can I butter a genuine
homemade croissant for your hungry friend down there?"

A tentative giggle fluttered in Eden's chest. Her mouth
tightened, then twitched. Tears scalded her eyes as she broke
into helpless laughter.

"I...I'm sorry..." she gasped. "Travis, this is too much.
I don't know what to say."

"That's easy enough. Say you'll give this crazy thing a
chance. Say you'll go to the reunion with me."

"No." She froze as if he had pressed a switch. "Not the
reunion. We settled that issue with the horse bet."

"We settled the truck issue. The reunion is still open."

Eden glared at him. "Save your breath. I'd rather jump
into boiling oil."

"Why?" he asked with an innocence that made Eden
want to punch him.

"You know why. One step into that gym, and I'll be right
back in high school. No one cared about me then. Why
should things be any different now?"

"Because you're a beautiful, intelligent, charming woman
who's gone out into the world and made something of herself."

"That's a joke, Travis. I may have changed on the surface, but inside, I'm the same person I always was."

"Have some coffee." He unscrewed the top of a small
thermos and trickled steaming liquid into the eggshell-thin
cups. Then he split one of the croissants, buttered both
halves, added a dab of marmalade and offered one piece to
her.

"Thank you." Eden nibbled at the warm flaky crust and
sipped the coffee, the fragile antique cup cradled between

her hands like a porcelain flower. A fish broke the surface of the reservoir, the splash of its silver body leaving rings of sunlit ripples.

"Utah native cutthroat," Travis said. "Great little fighters. Next time we come up here, I'll pack some fishing gear."

"Next time?" A knot of anxiety tightened in her stomach.

"Eden, what are you afraid of?"

"Wanting something too much." The truth spilled out of her lips before she could call it back. "Wanting something too much and never getting it."

"And what is it you want?" He had put down his coffee and was gazing at her with eyes that demanded answers.

You, she almost said, knowing it was true. Knowing that the old high-school dream still burned inside her. Knowing that all she had ever truly wanted was to have this man's love forever.

And knowing it was impossible.

"Happiness," she answered, masking the truth with something that was easier to express. "That's what I want. But it's a wish, not an expectation. Life becomes easier, I've discovered, if you don't ask for too much."

"Are you happy right now?"

"I...don't know." Eden stared into her coffee, eyes tracing the thin band of gold around the rim of the cup. "Happiness is more than a summer morning in the mountains, with birds singing, trout jumping and a breakfast fit for royalty."

"Is it?" His warm dark eyes looked into hers, penetrating her defenses, leaving her naked and quivering inside. "I'd call that a pretty good definition myself. Why wouldn't you?"

Eden flung the last bit of her croissant at his chest. "Hey, I thought you brought me up here to relax! This is turning into a philosophical discussion."

"So?" He finished his coffee and put the cup down on top of the picnic hamper. "Look, I'm trying very hard to find out what makes Eden Harper tick, and just when I think I'm making some headway, you turn evasive on me."

"Why should you care what makes me tick?"

"Do you really want to know?" His eyes had turned subtly dangerous, shattering Eden's hard-won composure.

"Have a strawberry!" Feigning playfulness, she snatched up a scarlet berry and shoved it into his mouth.

Surprised at her sudden action, he downed the berry and plucked a grape from the bowl. "So you want to play games, do you? Well, now it's your turn!"

He made a move toward her with the grape. Reflexively Eden jerked backward. The coffee flew out of her cup, splattering onto the pristine whiteness of the linen tablecloth.

"Oh, no!" Moisture blurred her eyes as she stared at the long brown stain. "Travis, I'm so sorry."

"Hey, it'll wash." He patted her shoulder. "As an old bachelor, I've gotten pretty good at laundry over the years. A little stain remover and it'll be as good as new."

"But it was your mother's."

"What's a tablecloth for? Don't worry about it." He caught her chin, turning her face toward him. Only then did he notice the tears.

"Oh, blast it, Eden, what's wrong? It can't just be the coffee..."

"Please," she whispered. "I know you mean well, but let's just finish this lovely breakfast and go. I can't handle any more of this, Travis. I need to get home and back to work."

He hesitated. Then something hard slid into place behind his eyes. "All right," he said, his voice emotionless. "Here, I'll pour you some more coffee."

They finished eating in awkward silence. Eden battled more tears as she helped Travis gather up the remains of their breakfast and load it into the back of the truck. It wasn't as if they'd quarreled. It wasn't as if they'd agreed that this was the end of the relationship. But somehow she knew it was.

Travis had done his best to win her favor. But he was a proud man, and she had slammed the door in his face one time too many. He would not try to open it again.

"Uh, about Fish Lake," she ventured as he boosted her into the cab. "Maybe it would be just as well if you asked someone else to go."

"There's plenty of time for that. Fasten your seat belt." He closed the door and walked around to the other side of the truck. His eyes stared straight through the windshield as he maneuvered the rough winding road down the mountain. Eden gazed wretchedly out the side window, wishing they *had* quarreled. At least it might have cleared the air and left some understanding between them.

But why was she complaining? She had known all along how the relationship would end. She had known the ending would hurt.

She just hadn't known how much.

Once, and then again, Eden cleared her throat to speak, but her churning thoughts refused to be formed into words. She sat in miserable silence, berating herself for her own foolishness.

How could she have let it happen—falling in love with Travis again after all these years? The relationship was as hopeless now as it had been in high school. Even if she stayed in town and tried to make things work, his interest was bound to fade. One day he would look at her and see that she had nothing to offer a man like him. And then . . . No, it would be wiser to let it die now, before the pain destroyed her.

"I hope you won't mind a quick detour by way of the ranch," he said, breaking the silence as the truck swung onto the main road. "I promised Nicole we'd go shopping

in Richfield after I picked her up at your house. But first,
need to run by and check on Chocolate. Her foal isn't du
for another couple of weeks, but this morning I notice
some waxing."

"Waxing?"

"Her teats are leaking colostrum," Travis explained as i
he were talking to a stranger. "The stuff looks like wa
where it dries on the insides of her hind legs. It's generall
the first sign that a mare's getting ready to foal."

Eden remembered the velvet-eyed mare Travis had bre
with Storm Cloud. She remembered his high hopes for thei
offspring, and now she felt his concern. "How long does
usually take mares to give birth?" she asked, pushing he
own troubles aside.

"From the time they start waxing? Hours. Even days
Since it's Chocolate's first foal, I expect she'll take plenty o
time. All the same, I'd like to make sure she's all right. Yo
don't mind, do you? I know you're anxious to get home…"

"It's fine. I can wait a few minutes."

"Thanks." His mouth smiled, but not his eyes. "Thi
won't take long, I promise. You'll be back at your editing i
no time."

Travis took a back road to the ranch. The truck flew alon
between patchwork fields of alfalfa, beets and potatoes, th
tires kicking up a long plume of dust. A cock pheasant ex
ploded out of the barrow pit and vanished over a barbed
wire fence. The sky was the clear hot blue of summer.

Eden had biked this road countless times, pedaling unt
the sweat dripped off the end of her nose. She had breathe
the sweetness of hay dust and damp earth, and splashed he
salty face with irrigation water from the canal. And all th
while, she had fantasized about Travis.

She had pictured him riding toward her on horseback. Sh
had imagined herself suddenly, miraculously beautiful—an
Travis looking down at her, knowing even then that she wa
the one.

Eden's thoughts scattered as the truck pulled through the gate of the ranch and crunched up the graveled drive. She could see horses grazing in the paddock behind the stable. On the porch, the two dogs had pricked up their ears. They came trotting down the steps to greet Travis as he opened the door and vaulted out of the driver's seat.

"Hang on," he said, glancing at Eden. "Chocolate's in her stall. I'll check her and be right back."

He sprinted toward the stable, leaving Eden to wonder if he was worried about the mare or just anxious to get her home and end the whole miserable morning. It was just as well, she told herself. She was all wrong for a man like Travis. No matter how she might love him, she didn't know how to be a rancher's wife. She didn't know how to cook or garden or put up peach preserves. She didn't even like horses, for heaven's sake!

The young Labrador padded over to the truck, sniffed the tires and left its calling card on one muddy hubcap. Then, seeing Eden, it stood on its hind legs and thrust its sleek black muzzle above the edge of the open window, begging for attention.

"Hello there, boy." Eden sighed as she scratched the satiny ears. Wistfully she scanned the green lawn in front of the house, wondering how the place might have looked with a bright red swing set and—

"Eden!"

Travis had burst out of the stable and was pounding toward the truck. Seeing the stark concern in his face, Eden flung open the door and sprang down to meet him.

"It's Chocolate," he said. "She's in trouble, and the vet's gone out of town for the weekend. I'm going to need your help. Sorry, but there's no one else to—"

"It's all right. I'm coming." She had to double-step to keep pace with his long stride.

"I don't understand it." Travis's words jerked out as he ran. "I've never seen a mare go into labor that fast. This morning I could've sworn—"

"What's the matter with her?"

"The foal—it's not coming." They rounded the entrance to the stable. The oversize-stall gate stood ajar. Eden glimpsed the mare lying on the straw inside, her belly a bulging, straining, mound of flesh.

"What do you want me to do?" Eden whispered, cold with fear.

"I've got to check and see how the foal's positioned. I'll need you to hold her head down and keep her calm. Can you do that?"

"I'll...have to." Eden felt light-headed. She gripped the side of the stall, gathering her courage as Travis raced to the tack room and came back tugging a long-sleeved rubber surgical glove onto his right hand.

"Ready?"

Eden nodded, praying she wouldn't faint. As Travis positioned himself to check the foal, she sank into the straw and gathered the massive, elegantly sculpted head into her lap. "Easy, Chocolate," she murmured, as her hand stroked the straining neck. "Easy, girl. It's all right. We won't hurt you."

Chocolate snorted and rolled her eyes, but she was not hard to hold. She seemed to realize, somehow, that these two puny humans were trying to help her.

Eden could not see what Travis was doing, but he talked as he worked. "I'm feeling a nose—that's excellent—and a little foreleg...just one, and— Uh-oh. There's the trouble."

"Bad?" Eden's voice was a shaky whisper.

"Not as bad as it could be. One leg's hung up in there. I'm going to have to maneuver it forward." He wiped the sweat from his forehead with his left sleeve. "Hold her tight. If she jerks, it could hurt her or the foal."

His eyes met Eden's over the body of the mare. In their warm depths she read trust, hope and, incredibly, love. Eden's heart contracted, and in that instant she realized there was nothing on earth she would not do for Travis Conroy.

"Ready?" he asked, crouching low again.

"Hang on a second." She bellied down in the straw and wrapped both arms around the mare's neck. Her fear was gone. In its place was a quiet concern, a deep need to help this beautiful animal and the man whose dreams rode her fate.

Eden pressed her cheek against the mare's warm satiny neck. "Ready!" she answered. Then, closing her eyes, she hung on with all her strength.

Travis prayed silently as he worked. One wrong move could rupture the mare or injure the foal's leg so badly that the little creature would have to be destroyed. His hand would have to be rock steady, his touch sensitive and sure.

Eden's presence in the stall was as sweet as a guardian angel's. He could hear her husky voice calming the mare. He could feel her spirit laboring with his own, and suddenly the rightness of it struck him with a force that almost brought tears to his eyes. This was what he wanted—Eden beside him, working, dreaming, sharing, loving. Eden with him forever.

He had all but abandoned hope back there on the mountain. He had told himself to forget her, to let her go back to New York where she belonged. But now he knew he could not give up so easily. If he wanted a life with Eden, he would have to lay his pride on the line one more time.

And as the foal's fragile leg slipped miraculously into position, Travis knew exactly what he had to do.

"What do you think?" he asked loudly enough that she would be sure to hear. "Boy or girl?"

She hesitated, but only for the space of a heartbeat. "Boy. Only a male would be so much trouble."

"Care to make a little wager?"

"You and your wagers! You've already discovered what the foal is, haven't you?"

"Nope. Cross my heart. Just to prove it, you can bet either way. But I get to name the stakes."

"Stakes?" Eden groaned. "Do I even need to ask?"

"Smart lady." Travis peeled off the rubber glove and eased wearily to his feet. "We've done all we can. It's time to get out of the way and let nature take its course."

Eden was lying in the straw, one arm still embracing the mare's neck. Her hair was tousled, her face flushed and damp. Bits of yellow straw clung to her jeans and T-shirt.

She had never looked more beautiful.

"Boy or girl? You call it." Travis reached out, clasped her free hand and pulled her up. She was trembling, her legs so unsteady she could barely stand. He circled her waist with his arm and drew her close against his side. Her head nestled in the curve of his throat, their bodies fitting as if they had been fashioned for each other.

"If I guess right, you'll never mention that reunion to me again. Agreed?"

"Agreed. And if you guess wrong—"

"I know." Her finger toyed with a button on his shirt. "I'll take my medicine like a big girl and—" Eden's breath caught as she watched the mare. "Travis, it's happening!"

Chocolate's head was up now, ears pricked, eyes alert. Her body strained as she pushed the small new life into the world.

"This is incredible." Eden clung to him, tears of emotion wetting his shirt as the foal tumbled onto the straw, still shrouded in its glistening birth sac.

"I know," he whispered, his chin stirring the pale silk of her hair. "It's a fresh miracle every time you see it. Come on now, what'll it be?"

Chocolate was cleaning the foal now, her big pink tongue licking and licking. Travis held his breath as he waited for Eden to answer. A lifetime with this woman would be heaven—but there was no hope for that unless she could be happy here in the little town where she had once been so miserable.

He wanted Eden more than he had ever wanted anything in his life. But unless she could come to terms with Edna Rae, she was better off in New York.

The reunion, he told himself, was the key to everything.

"No more stalling," he teased, grateful she could not see his face. "Boy or girl?"

Her body tensed against him. "Boy—no, girl. I'll go with girl."

"You're sure?"

"I'm sure."

"Okay, it's a bet. Let's watch."

The mare was on her feet now, her foal stirring to life under its mother's vigorous cleaning. Its delicate head quivered and jerked upward, large velvety eyes blinking in the morning shadows. Travis's throat tightened as he picked out the silvery coat, tapered muzzle and flaring nostrils that were unmistakable marks of Storm Cloud's bloodline.

"He—she's beautiful," Eden whispered.

"So are you." He kissed her then, love and tenderness bursting inside him. Her lips were salty with tears. They molded warmly to his as she softened in his arms.

Travis held her close, tasting the silky heaven of her mouth, her cheeks, her closed eyelids. His whole being ached with the desire to pour out his heart to her, stripping away everything between them but the truth. But he knew it was too soon. He could not risk pushing her too hard. Not yet.

The foal was already fighting to stand. One wobbly leg unfolded and braced, then two more. For a perilous instant it balanced, then toppled into the straw, only to struggle to its feet again. Chocolate nickered and nuzzled her baby. Instinctively the foal tottered beneath her belly. Its nose butted the swollen teats. Then it was sucking, its stringy tail whipping back and forth like a metronome gone berserk. What Travis glimpsed beneath it showed the little creature to be unmistakably male.

Relief eased out of him in a long sigh. He had gambled everything on this bet with Eden, but the odds of winning had been no better than even. It was a good sign.

He teased her eyebrow with a nibbling kiss. "There's no delicate way to put this, but if you look carefully between our young friend's legs, you'll see that you just lost your wager."

She sagged against him with a moan of dismay. Travis felt his heart sink, but he hugged her good-naturedly, biting back his disappointment. "Looks like everything's under control," he said, "but *I* won't be for long, unless we hightail it out of here. Come on, we'd better be getting you home."

She pushed away from him, leaving an empty ache where her warmth had been. "You're right. Nicole will be wondering what happened to us."

"And she'll be anxious to see the foal." Travis turned away to close the stall door, realizing that for now, at least, he'd taken things as far as he dared. "Time to go," he said, risking a playful swat at her firm rump. "Let's move it, city lady."

Eden left the window down, letting the dry summer wind tangle her hair. Her fingers toyed restlessly with the seat belt, echoing emotions that rose and tumbled like chips in a millrace.

Travis's knuckle brushed her thigh as he reached for the gearshift knob. The fleeting touch went through her like a warm current, triggering the memory of his arms, his sweet searching mouth and the fresh realization that she belonged with this man.

Fantasies swirled in her mind—new fantasies to replace the old ones. The red swing set in the yard. Long winter nights snuggling in front of the fieldstone fireplace. Welcoming Nicole every summer. Watching the birth of spring foals. Watching children grow up.

But what was she thinking? There was the town. The reunion—

"So, what shall we name the little fellow?" Travis asked pleasantly.

Eden blinked, then realized he was talking about the foal. "You're asking *me?*"

"Why not? You helped bring him into the world."

Eden's mind had gone blank. "Uh, why don't we let Nicole name him? It might make up for her missing out on his birth."

"Nicole's named other foals. This one's yours." His gaze warmed her to the soles of her feet. Eden quivered with the wonder of it, suddenly afraid. Happiness was too perilous, too easily snatched out of reach. She closed her eyes, knowing the fragility of dreams as the truck pulled up to the house and Travis came around to open her door.

"I won't invite myself in," he said, his touch lingering as he helped her out of the cab. "We've both got a lot of thinking to do."

"I...I'll send Nicole out," Eden murmured, turning away in flustered confusion. "Tell her how much I appreciate her staying."

As he closed the door, she started up the driveway. Only then did she realize he had said something else.

"What?" She paused, glancing back to meet his mischievous smile.

"I said, you're going to be the prettiest girl at the reunion."

"Oh, you—"

"I'll call you!" He grinned as he vaulted back into the cab.

Eden flounced up to the house, although she wasn't really angry. Teasing was Travis's mask; she understood that now. Behind it, he was as scared and unsure about their relationship as she was.

All the more reason to love him.

The front door was unlocked. Eden brushed the straw off her jeans as she walked into the entry. "Nicole, I'm back, and your dad's waiting," she called. "Thanks for..."

Her voice dried up in her throat as she saw Nicole huddled on the stairway, staring down at her with accusing eyes.

Clutched in her arms was Eden's high-school yearbook.

Chapter Ten

Eden stood in the open doorway, sick with dismay. "Nicole," she whispered, "where did you—"

"I found it, all right? Your mother was taking a nap and got bored." Nicole rose slowly and glided down the stairs, still clutching the yearbook to her chest. Her wounded angry eyes never left Eden's face. "That girl," she said, "the one who wrote those awful letters to my father. Her name wasn't Agnes. It was Edna. Edna Rae. It was you."

"Nicole, that was a long time ago—"

"You lied to me," she said in a flat little voice. "That first day, driving home from the airport, you told me you didn't know her."

"I'm sorry." Eden felt as small as a toad. She squirmed under the torture of Nicole's cold scrutiny. "I was embarrassed. I didn't know what else to say."

"You could have told me the truth. It was no big deal. I would've laughed. I would've liked you even more for it. Instead, you lied. You lied, and you never let me know."

"Nicole—" Eden felt her dreams shredding like tissue banners in a summer storm.

"I trusted you, Eden. I thought you were my friend."

"I am your friend." It was a useless argument, Eden knew.

"Friends don't lie to each other." Nicole shoved the yearbook into Eden's hands and stalked out of the house, clicking the door behind her like an angry exclamation point.

Shattered, Eden sagged onto the bottom step. She huddled there, listening to the purr of Travis's truck as it pulled away and vanished around the corner. So much for dreams she told herself. So much for red swing sets and long snuggly evenings. Nicole despised her. She was probably venting her contempt right now, telling Travis how Eden Harper had lied through her sneaky conniving teeth.

And it wouldn't matter what Travis thought of the story. He would not risk alienating his beloved daughter for any woman on earth.

Edna Rae had triumphed again.

"Is that you, dear?" Her mother's sleepy voice echoed down the stairs. "I thought I heard the door."

"It's me—I." Eden edited her own reply as she trudged up the steps, the yearbook dangling from her hand.

"So, how was the ride?" Madge was sitting up, cheek blossom pink from her nap. "Did you have a good time?"

"It was...fine. Nice truck." Eden sank dejectedly onto a corner of the hand-quilted satin bedspread. "How was Nicole?"

"Oh, we had a delightful visit. She's a charming child—so polite and thoughtful. And she absolutely worships you. Did you know that?"

Eden swallowed a moan.

"She told me that meeting you had started her thinking about her own future. When she finishes school, she wants to go to New York and study flute at Julliard. She even

ked me if you'd mind picking her up some application
aterials when you get back to..."

Madge's words and smile faded as her sharp blue eyes
anned Eden's face. "Sweetheart, what is it? Has some-
ng happened?"

Eden shook her hair in too-vehement denial. "Nothing's
ppened. Nothing that I...won't get over."

"Tell me about it." The soft-spoken command nudged
en over the brink of her own composure. The breath
:cupped out of her as she collapsed into a disconsolate
ap at the foot of the bed.

"I love him, Mom," she whispered. "I've loved him since
was fourteen years old. And it's hopeless. Just plain
peless!"

"Are you certain?" Madge's sure fingers massaged
en's shoulder, soothing away knots of tension. "Travis
·uldn't keep coming around if he didn't care for you."

"Travis isn't the problem. Travis is wonderful. He's so
·nderful I can scarcely believe he's real."

"Then what is it?" Madge asked gently. "Is it the town?"

Eden took a ragged breath, forcing herself at last to face
e truth. "No," she said slowly, "it isn't the town. This is
ine town, filled with compassionate caring people."

"Then what is it, dear?"

"Don't you see?" Eden sat up, fingers raking the tan-
:d hair back from her face. "It's *me*—it's Edna Rae. I've
ent the past eleven years trying to get away from her, but
:ry time I come home—"

"Now, what's so awful about Edna Rae?" Madge caught
r daughter's hand, imprisoning Eden's fingers in her
rm clasp. "I, for one, remember Edna Rae very fondly.
emember her as the sweet little baby I named after my
·n mother. I remember her as a young girl growing up, so
ght and eager to learn, and such a comfort to me after her
her died."

"Oh, Mom." Eden could not stop the rush of tears t|
flooded her eyes and trickled down her cheeks. She wo|
have flung her arms around her mother, but at that m|
ment the telephone shrilled from the downstairs hallw|
Propelled by reflex, she bolted off the bed.

"I'll get it. It's probably Rob." She raced down the st|
and flung herself at the receiver.

"Hello."

"Panting as usual, are you?" Travis's voice was a s|
sual tickling caress that sent each spoken syllable quiver|
along the inner curl of Eden's ear. As strength deserted |
knees, she leaned her back against the wall for support, t|
slid slowly to the floor.

"Are you all right?" he asked, reading her silence.

Eden gulped back a hiccup. "Ask your daughter."

"What?" He paused, then chuckled. "Oh, the yearbo|
thing. Don't worry, she'll get over it."

"Get over it?" Eden stared down at the worn tweed c|
pet, dumbfounded that he would take the disaster so ca|
ally. "You didn't see the way she looked at me—so hurt a|
betrayed, as if she'd never forgive me. Travis, I...I can't |
you again. I can't come between you and your daughter. |

"Oh, for the love of..." He muttered a few choice cur|
under his breath. "Eden, I know that look of hers. And |
had a dime for every time Nicole's turned it on *me,* I co|
buy a gold-plated horse trailer as long as an Amtrak car. |
for the rest, I can't force you to go on seeing me, but th|
is the small matter of our wager..."

Eden's heart quivered, then sank like a plumb bob. "Y|
really intend to hold me to that silly bet?"

"You're damned right I do."

Fear twisted its knot around her ribs. "Trust me, Trav|
You don't want to walk into that reunion with Edna R|
Harper on your arm."

"I want to walk in with *you* on my arm, whatever the hell ur name happens to be that night." His voice crackled like tic over the line. "Is that clear?"

Eden clutched the phone, startled by his vehemence, but t cowed. "And if I simply refuse to go?" she challenged n.

"Let's put it this way." His voice had gone as thin and rd as barbed wire. "I'll be showing up on your doorstep seven-fifteen on the night of July fifth. If you're not dy to go with me, you'll find out what happens to ladies no welsh on their bets!"

"Am I to take that as a threat?" Eden had meant the estion to sound coldly defiant, but the last word emerged a nervous croak. So much for cool.

"Take it any way you want, city lady." Travis's own mposure was like the smooth white side of a refrigerator.

"Do you have anything else to say?" she demanded ffly.

There was a long silence on the line—a silence Eden ached fill with apologies, heartfelt promises and all the loving ords she'd held back for sixteen years. But a lump of pride d fear blocked her throat. She could not speak.

"We both seem to have said enough." His voice rasped to the stillness. "See you on the fifth, all right?"

Eden's lips moved, but no sound emerged. She cradled the one numbly against her cheek, listening to the click as he ng up, followed by the mechanical buzz on the empty line.

Battling despair, she struggled to her feet and replaced the ceiver on its hook. July fifth loomed like a sinister cloud, rtending the blackest night of her life. Not only would she facing classmates she'd never wanted to see again, she uld also be spending the entire evening with Travis. And nsidering the strain that hung between them like a cur-in of icicles, the reunion promised to be one long night-are.

Get out of town—that would be the smart thing to c
Call the airline. Schedule her return flight for July four
or sooner, so that when Travis came by—

But what was she thinking? Madge would need her he
for the next couple of weeks at least. She couldn't just r
off and leave her mother lying helpless in bed.

Eden sighed as she trooped back up the stairs. She w
stuck right here, she conceded, with no escape in sight.

And heaven help her if she wasn't ready when Tra
showed up to escort her to the reunion.

The rest of the week dragged by with no word from t
ranch. When she wasn't helping her mother, Eden spent l
time hunched over the kitchen table, red-lining the ne
batch of manuscripts Gordon had mailed her from N
York. Her left eye developed a twitch from the strain, a
she had to abandon her contacts for the old horn-rimm
glasses she'd kept since high school. The bathroom mirr
confirmed that her roots were growing in, their natural col
a mousy dishwater blond. A solitary zit had popped out
her chin.

No doubt about it, she concluded glumly. She was tur
ing back into Edna Rae.

By July fourth, Madge was feeling well enough to ri
short distances in the car. That morning, Rob took her
watch the parade in Richfield. Declining their invitation
come along, Eden shut herself up in the kitchen with P:
nell's new sixth-grade math course and a big pitcher of ic
tea. No way, she vowed, was she setting foot outside t
door today.

She was just starting on the second chapter when h
concentration was shattered by a muffled thumping at t
kitchen window. She glanced up to see a long brown fa
gazing at her through the glass.

A squeak of fear escaped her lips before she realized s
was seeing a horse—a horse in the backyard.

Only after she'd burst onto the back porch, slamming the
screen behind her, did Eden recognize Tucker. He had lowered his head to graze, his big yellow teeth cropping healthy
hunks of the back lawn. On his bare back, perched like a
brown pixie, sat Nicole.

"Uh, hi." Eden reached out a tentative hand and patted
the big gelding's shoulder. "I thought you'd be watching the
parade."

"Parades are for kids." She stared down at Eden, her face
unreadable.

"If you've come to visit my mother, I'm afraid she's
gone."

"That's okay. I came to see you."

"Oh." Eden swallowed her apprehension. "In that case,
would you like to get down and come in?" she asked cautiously. "There's some ice cream in the fridge."

Nicole shook her dark curls. "I'd better stay on Tucker.
He likes to roam around and sometimes he gets into trouble."

"Does your father know you're here?"

"No." Nicole brushed a fly off Tucker's rump. "My
dad's busy shoveling out the stable. He said it seemed like
the appropriate thing to do this morning." She cleared her
throat as if she was about to make a speech. "Eden, my
dad's been bummed out all week. I've never seen him like
this."

Squinting behind her glasses, Eden gazed up at Travis's
daughter. "Are you saying it's my fault?" she asked,
squeezing the words from her aching throat.

"I think my dad's afraid. He wants things to work out
with you and he's scared they won't." Nicole inspected a
freckle on the back of her wrist. "I think he's afraid you
won't go to the reunion with him, and that will be the end
of everything."

"The end of everything." Eden repeated the word weaving her own anguish into each syllable. "But isn't th what you want? I thought you didn't like me, Nicole."

"Ha!" Her explosive little chuckle was a poignant ec of Travis's. "If I didn't like you, I would never have gott so mad. My dad calls it shooting from the hip, and I do i lot, especially with people I care about. I'm sorry, Eden.

"I'm sorry, too." Eden felt something break loose in l chest, choking her voice with sudden emotion. "I'll nev lie again, to you, or your father, or—"

"Ooh!" Nicole grimaced adorably. "We're getting a fully mushy here, aren't we? Golly gee, I'd better be goi before things get out of control!" She swung Tucker ba toward the driveway. "If my dad calls, you haven't se me!"

"I said I wasn't going to lie!" Eden shouted after her, b Nicole was already headed for the corner at a trot, the cl ter of Tucker's shod hooves echoing down the street.

Eden stood gazing after her, an uncertain smile tuggi at a corner of her mouth. They were a pair, Travis and l daughter—spirited, magnetic and irresistible. Golden, as s would never be.

Slowly she walked back into the kitchen, Nicole's wor echoing in her mind.

He's afraid you won't go to the reunion with him, a that will be the end of everything.

The end of everything.

Suddenly Eden was rummaging in the kitchen drawer 1 the phone book, her fingers riffling furiously through pages. She knew today was a holiday and no one was like to answer her call, but this was an emergency. She cou only pray that Marvella Johnson, her mother's hairdress would have an answering machine—and an opening for 1 morrow morning.

* * *

The doorbell chimed once, then again. Almost forgetting to breathe, Eden hurried down the stairs to answer it. Travis had not called her since the day the foal was born. But it was the fifth of July, the time precisely seven-fifteen, and she knew he was a man of his word.

She opened the door to see him standing in the blue twilight, his long fingers fiddling with the knot of his burgundy silk tie. He looked as nervous as a high-school sophomore picking up his first prom date, but when he saw her, his face warmed in a heart-melting smile.

"You look beautiful," he said, his gaze taking in the honey-gold swirl of her hair and the pale green silk sheath that matched her eyes. "I'll confess, I didn't know what to expect. Curlers and face cream, a gorilla suit, a Playboy bunny outfit..."

"Would you like to come in?" she asked. "Mom and Rob are out somewhere watching the moon come up."

He laughed, white teeth flashing against his golden skin. "Oh, no, you don't! I know your game, city lady. Lure me inside with a come-hither look and a bit of bubbly, and while you're having your way with me, I'll forget all about the reunion."

"You see right through me, don't you?" Eden faked a laugh, wishing she *had* thought of such a plan. "For that matter, there's a pretty good 'Star Trek' rerun on channel 13, the one where the *Enterprise* is invaded by amazon warriors in little feather bikinis. Are you sure you wouldn't like to—"

"Come on!" He caught her waist, swung her off her feet, and swept her to the truck. "You're going to the reunion, Miss Eden Harper—that is, if I can keep my hands off you long enough to drive that far!"

He deposited her firmly on the seat, shut the door and strode around to the driver's side. Eden closed her eyes, her heart slamming against her ribs like a wrecking ball. She wasn't up to tonight, she realized. She had wanted to do this for Travis—wanted it badly enough to have her hair done, put on her favorite dress and risk the twitch by wearing her contacts. But it wasn't going to work. The thought of walking into that gymnasium was as chilling as a plunge into a snake-infested sinkhole.

"The ball awaits you, Cinderella!" Travis gunned the engine and the truck shot out of the driveway. Eden clutched her seat belt as panic climbed the walls of her throat. Her searching eyes found Travis in the dim light of the cab. Aching with love, she traced his rugged profile, eyes lingering on the sensual curve of his lips, on his strong supple hands.

He's afraid you won't go to the reunion with him, and that will be the end of everything.

Ahead, she could see the high school, the roof of the gym a looming block against the sunset. The parking lot was filled with cars and the dark shapes of people funneling toward the brightly lit doors.

"Are you all right?" Travis's hand brushed hers as he swung off the street. His fingers were warm. Hers, she realized, were icicles. She nodded mutely, feeling like Marie Antoinette on her way to the guillotine.

He parked the truck, then came around to help her down from the cab. Dizzy with anxiety, Eden forced herself to take his arm. It was all right, she reassured herself frantically. She was with Travis. She could do this for him.

Then she heard the music.

The scratchy recording blared out of the gym like a poignant cry, summoning a rush of memories. The Friday-afternoon dances. The interminable torture of sitting on the sidelines, alone and unwanted, watching the golden people dance past her. The slow shattering of her heart...

The song was "Endless Love."

Eden sagged against the front fender of the pickup. "Travis, I can't do it," she whispered. "Please don't make me go in there. All those people..."

"They're only human, Eden. Just like everybody else in this world." He kept walking, tugging her arm as he moved ahead.

"No." She pulled away from him. "You don't understand. It's not them. It's me."

"You?" He turned back toward her then, his eyes blazing a desperate fire she had never seen before. "And who are you tonight? Can you answer that one?"

"Travis..." She took a step backward, but he caught her chin with his hand, forcing her to look straight into his face.

"I have a confession to make," he said, a thread of steel in his voice. "I seem to have fallen in love with two women. One of them is dazzling and sophisticated, with enough self-confidence to take on the whole world. The other—" his thumb stroked her cheek "—the other is shy and deep and sensitive—and tender."

A tear pooled its way along the side of Eden's nose. An aching lump rose in her throat as she gazed up at him, afraid to believe what she was hearing.

"I love both of them," he said, "because it takes both Eden and Edna Rae to make *you.*" He skimmed away her tear with a fingertip. "I want to give us a chance," he said. "I want to take what we've got and build it into something that will last a lifetime. But there's one condition. Unless you can walk into that reunion—unless you can face Edna Rae and embrace her as the wonderful vital part of you she is—we might as well shake hands and say goodbye right now."

Eden looked up into his dark brown eyes. She saw the hope there. She saw the love, the dreams, the fear; and she knew what she had to do.

Closing her eyes for an instant, she took a long breath, all but draining the well of her courage. Then she slipped her cold fingers into Travis's big warm hand. "Come on," she whispered, trembling like an aspen leaf. "Let's go inside."

The gym looked exactly as she remembered it. Crepe-paper streamers in red and white—the school colors—fluttered from the ceiling. Red and white helium balloons floated from wherever their strings could be anchored. Dots of red and white confetti speckled jackets, dresses and hair.

The stereo speakers rocked with the driving beat of AC/DC blasting out "You Shook Me All Night Long." Eden clung to Travis's arm, feeling as if she had stepped into a time warp.

But it was only an illusion.

"Travis, old pal!" The man striding toward them had thinning brown hair and wore wire-framed glasses. A saggy paunch strained the buttons of his white shirt above his belt. "And who's this? Good gosh, I can't believe it! It's Edna Rae Harper!"

"LeRoy." Travis pumped the man's hand as Eden fought the urge to stare. LeRoy Hatch, captain of the football team. One of the golden people.

"Edna Rae!" he exclaimed again. "I hear you went to New York and made it big. Hell, I'm glad somebody did! Me, I married a girl from Beaver and took over her dad's Chevy dealership. It's not the NFL, but who's complaining? Sure is good to see you! Hey—isn't that Mitzi Cole over there?"

"Mitzi Cole Davenport Davies." Travis nodded toward the former cheerleader, who was prancing to the beat in a black spandex jumpsuit. "Runs a health club in Phoenix. She's been through two husbands—told me she hangs on to their names because she didn't get much else."

"Gutsy kid, that Mitz," LeRoy commented. "Say, isn't that Lynette headed our way?"

Eden's head swiveled so fast it almost snapped her neck. The prom queen's long auburn curls were as luxuriant as ever. As for the rest of her—

"Hi, you guys!" Lynette waddled toward them, enormously pregnant beneath a flowered tent of a dress with a white lace collar. "Can you believe this? I'm due in ten days—the doctor says it's twins! And I wanted to be so glamorous for this reunion. Talk about timing—" Her smile broadened as she approached Eden and enfolded her in a warm hug. "Hey, I'm so glad you came, Eden—Eden! I talk to your mother at church every week. She's so proud of you. We all are. Gosh, you were always so smart. You don't know how I used to envy your brains!"

"And I always envied your beauty." Eden returned the hug a little self-consciously. "It's great to see you, Lynette. Congratulations on your twins."

Eden stood in the curve of Travis's arm as the prom queen tottered off to greet skinny bookish Cecil Higby, who sported an Armani suit and an exotic Japanese wife. "I feel like such an idiot," she whispered. "Everybody's changed. They're all so..."

"So human?" Travis laughed as he swung her against him. "Come on, I want to dance with my girl."

Someone had changed the record. The rich mellow voice of Kenny Rogers singing "Through the Years," floated across the gym. Eden stiffened against Travis as he steered her into the once-forbidden milieu of swaying couples. "I told you I couldn't dance," she protested.

"And I said you just needed the right teacher." He drew her against his chest. "Just snuggle up and move with me," he whispered in her ear. "You'll be fine."

The first few steps were awkward. Then Eden began to feel the music. She began to hear the words and sense the rhythm that flowed from Travis's lean warm body into hers. She closed her eyes, stretching a little to lay her temple against the curve of his clean-shaven jaw. His breath was a sensual whisper in her ear.

Through the years...

The feeling was heaven, she thought. Sweeter than her sweetest dream, more thrilling than her wildest romantic fantasy.

Eden Harper had come home at last.

Epilogue

Moonlight silvered the pale aspens and cast the pines into pools of inky shadow. The silken breeze was pungent with wood smoke and cool with the promise of autumn.

Eden stood on a sheltered third-floor balcony of the Brian Head Lodge, snuggled into Travis's soft fleece robe. The night was filled with peaceful sounds—the call of a bird, the sigh of the wind, the glassy tinkle of music from the hotel dining room somewhere below.

She closed her eyes, quivering with happiness as Travis's arms slipped around her from behind, pulling her against his solid warmth.

"So, what are you thinking, Mrs. Conroy?" His lips teased the back of her neck.

"I'm just thinking about today," she whispered, "trying to remember every lovely detail, so I can tell our children about it in the years to come."

"It was a grand double wedding." His hand lost itself in the fuzzy folds of the robe, gently exploring. "Two beautiful brides—"

"And two tall, dark, handsome bridegrooms—"

"And one little bridesmaid who was flirting with every male under the age of twenty five—"

"Oh, hush." Eden turned in his arms, lifting her face for his kiss. "Nicole's got a good head on her shoulders. She'll outgrow it."

"If we live that long!" He gathered her close, his lips and arms seeking what they both knew was soon to come. "I've got the fire going in there," he whispered. "Let's go inside and get warm."

"I'm pretty warm already!" She laughed as he scooped her up in his arms and carried her indoors, where the bed was already turned down and waiting. From the small brick fireplace, dancing flames cast their golden spell over the room.

He lowered her to the sheets, tugging away the robe to reveal the lacy white nightgown underneath. "I love you, Edna Rae," he murmured, his lips brushing her throat. "And I love you, too, Eden Harper Conroy."

Eden's fingers tangled in his thick dark hair, gently guiding his mouth to her breasts. She felt his breath catch, felt his arms slide around her, and then, with a sweetness beyond dreams, all her fantasies came true.

* * * * *

COMING NEXT MONTH

#1198 MAD FOR THE DAD—Terry Essig
Fabulous Fathers
He knew next to nothing about raising his infant nephew. So ingle "dad" Daniel Van Scott asked his lovely new neighbor Rachel Gatlin for a little advice—and found himself noticing her charms as both a mother...*and* as a woman.

#1199 HAVING GABRIEL'S BABY—Kristin Morgan
Bundles of Joy
One fleeting night of passion and Joelle was in the family way! And now the father of her baby, hardened rancher Gabriel Lafleur, insisted they marry immediately. But could they find true love before their bundle of joy arrived?

#1200 NEW YEAR'S WIFE—Linda Varner
Home for the Holidays
Years ago, the man Julie McCrae had loved declared her too young for him and walked out of her life. Now Tyler Jordan was back, and Julie was all woman. But did she dare hope that Tyler would renew the love they'd once shared, and make her his New Year's Wife?

#1201 FAMILY ADDITION—Rebecca Daniels
Single dad Colt Wyatt thought his little girl, Jenny, was all he needed in his life, until he met Cassandra Sullivan—the lovely woman who enchanted his daughter and warmed his heart. But after so long, would he truly learn to love again and make Cassandra an addition to his family?

#1202 ABOUT THAT KISS—Jayne Addison
Maid of honor Joy Mackey was convinced that Nick Tremain was out to ruin her sister's wedding. And she was determined to go to any lengths to see her sis happily wed—even if it meant keeping Nick busy by marrying him herself!

#1203 GROOM ON THE LOOSE—Christine Scott
To save him from scandal, Cassie Andrews agreed to pose as Greg Lawton's *pretend* significant other. The handsome doctor was surely too arrogant—and way too sexy—to be real husband material! Or was this groom just waiting to be tamed?

FAST CASH 4031 DRAW RULES
NO PURCHASE OR OBLIGATION NECESSARY

Fifty prizes of $50 each will be awarded in random drawings to be conducted no later than 3/28/97 from amongst all eligible responses to this prize offer received as of 2/14/97. To enter, follow directions, affix 1st-class postage and mail OR write Fast Cash 4031 on a 3" x 5" card along with your name and address and mail that card to: Harlequin's Fast Cash 4031 Draw, P.O. Box 1395, Buffalo, NY 14240-1395 OR P.O. Box 618, Fort Erie, Ontario L2A 5X3. (Limit: one entry per outer envelope; all entries must be sent via 1st-class mail.) Limit: one prize per household. Odds of winning are determined by the number of eligible responses received. Offer is open only to residents of the U.S. (except Puerto Rico) and Canada and is void wherever prohibited by law. All applicable laws and regulations apply. Any litigation within the province of Quebec respecting the conduct and awarding of a prize in this sweepstakes maybe submitted to the Régie des alcools, des courses et des jeux. In order for a Canadian resident to win a prize, that person will be required to correctly answer a time-limited arithmetical skill-testing question to be administered by mail. Names of winners available after 4/28/97 by sending a self-addressed, stamped envelope to: Fast Cash 4031 Draw Winners, P.O. Box 4200, Blair, NE 68009-4200.

OFFICIAL RULES
MILLION DOLLAR SWEEPSTAKES
NO PURCHASE NECESSARY TO ENTER

1. To enter, follow the directions published. Method of entry may vary. For eligibility, entries must be received no later than March 31, 1998. No liability is assumed for printing errors, lost, late, non-delivered or misdirected entries.

    To determine winners, the sweepstakes numbers assigned to submitted entries will be compared against a list of randomly pre-selected prize winning numbers. In the event all prizes are not claimed via the return of prize winning numbers, random drawings will be held from among all other entries received to award unclaimed prizes.

2. Prize winners will be determined no later than June 30, 1998. Selection of winning numbers and random drawings are under the supervision of D. L. Blair, Inc., an independent judging organization whose decisions are final. Limit: one prize to a family or organization. No substitution will be made for any prize, except as offered. Taxes and duties on all prizes are the sole responsibility of winners. Winners will be notified by mail. Odds of winning are determined by the number of eligible entries distributed and received.

3. Sweepstakes open to residents of the U.S. (except Puerto Rico), Canada and Europe who are 18 years of age or older, except employees and immediate family members of Torstar Corp., D. L. Blair, Inc., their affiliates, subsidiaries, and all other agencies, entities, and persons connected with the use, marketing or conduct of this sweepstakes. All applicable laws and regulations apply. Sweepstakes offer void wherever prohibited by law. Any litigation within the province of Quebec respecting the conduct and awarding of a prize in this sweepstakes must be submitted to the Régie des alcools, des courses et des jeux. In order to win a prize, residents of Canada will be required to correctly answer a time-limited arithmetical skill-testing question to be administered by mail.

4. Winners of major prizes (Grand through Fourth) will be obligated to sign and return an Affidavit of Eligibility and Release of Liability within 30 days of notification. In the event of non-compliance within this time period or if a prize is returned as undeliverable, D. L. Blair Inc. may at its sole discretion award that prize to an alternate winner. By acceptance of their prize, winners consent to use of their names, photographs or other likeness for purposes of advertising, trade and promotion on behalf of Torstar Corp., its affiliates and subsidiaries without further compensation unless prohibited by law. Torstar Corp. and D. L. Blair, Inc. their affiliates and subsidiaries are not responsible for errors in printing of sweepstakes and prizewinning numbers. In the event a duplication of a prizewinning number occurs, a random drawing will be held from among all entries received with that prizewinning number to award that prize.

5. This sweepstakes is presented by Torstar Corp., its subsidiaries and affiliates in conjunction with book, merchandise and/or product offerings. The number of prizes to be awarded and their value are as follows: Grand Prize — $1,000,000 (payable at $33,333.33 a year for 30 years); First Prize — $50,000; Second Prize — $10,000; Third Prize — $5,000; 3 Fourth Prizes — $1,000 each; 10 Fifth Prizes — $250 each; 1,000 Sixth Prizes — $10 each. Values of all prizes are in U.S. currency. Prizes in each level will be presented in different creative executions, including various currencies, vehicles, merchandise and travel. Any presentation of a prize level in a currency other than U.S. currency represents an approximate equivalent to the U.S. currency prize for that level, at that time. Prize winners will have the opportunity of selecting any prize offered for that level; however, the actual non U.S. currency equivalent prize, if offered and selected, shall be awarded at the exchange rate existing at 3:00 P.M. New York time on March 31, 1998. A travel prize option, if offered and selected by winner, must be completed within 12 months of selection and is subject to: traveling companion(s) completing and returning a Release of Liability prior to travel; and hotel and flight accommodations availability. For a current list of all prize options offered within prize levels, send a self-addressed, stamped envelope (WA residents need not affix postage) to: MILLION DOLLAR SWEEPSTAKES Prize Options, P.O. Box 4456, Blair, NE 68009-4456, USA.

6. For a list of prize winners (available after July 31, 1998) send a separate, stamped, self-addressed envelope to: MILLION DOLLAR SWEEPSTAKES Winners, P.O. Box 4459, Blair, NE 68009-4459, USA.

EXTRA BONUS PRIZE DRAWING
NO PURCHASE OR OBLIGATION NECESSARY TO ENTER

7. The Extra Bonus Prize will be awarded in a random drawing to be conducted no later than 5/30/98 from among all entries received. To qualify, entries must be received by 3/31/98 and comply with published directions. Prize ($50,000) is valued in U.S. currency. Prize will be presented in different creative expressions, including various currencies, vehicles, merchandise and travel. Any presentation in a currency other than U.S. currency represents an approximate equivalent to the U.S. currency value at that time. Prize winner will have the opportunity of selecting any prize offered in any presentation of the Extra Bonus Prize Drawing; however, the actual non U.S. currency equivalent prize, if offered and selected by winner, shall be awarded at the exchange rate existing at 3:00 P.M. New York time on March 31, 1998. For a current list of prize options offered, send a self-addressed, stamped envelope (WA residents need not affix postage) to: Extra Bonus Prize Options, P.O. Box 4462, Blair, NE 68009-4462, USA. All eligibility requirements and restrictions of the MILLION DOLLAR SWEEPSTAKES apply. Odds of winning are dependent upon number of eligible entries received. No substitution for prize except as offered. For the name of winner (available after 7/31/98), send a self-addressed, stamped envelope to: Extra Bonus Prize Winner, P.O. Box 4463, Blair, NE 68009-4463, USA.

SWP-S12ZD2

This holiday season,
Linda Varner brings three very special couples

HOME
FOR THE HOLIDAYS

where they discover the joy of love and family—
and the wonder of wedded bliss.

✽✽✽✽✽✽✽✽✽✽✽✽✽✽✽✽✽✽✽✽✽✽✽✽✽✽✽✽

WON'T YOU BE MY HUSBAND?—Lauren West and
Nick Gatewood never expected their family and friends to get
word of their temporary engagement and nonintended nuptials. Or
to find themselves falling in love with each other. Is that a *real*
wedding they're planning over Thanksgiving dinner?
(SR#1188, 11/96)

MISTLETOE BRIDE—There was plenty of room at Dani Sellica's
Colorado ranch for stranded holiday guests Ryan Given and his
young son. Until the mistletoe incident! Christmas morning brought
presents from ol' Saint Nick...but would it also bring wedding bells?
(SR#1193, 12/96)

NEW YEAR'S WIFE—Eight years after Tyler Jordan and
Julie McCrae shared a passionate kiss at the stroke of midnight,
Tyler is back and Julie is certain he doesn't fit into her plans for
wedded bliss. But does his plan to prove her wrong include a lifetime
of New Year's kisses? (SR#1200, 1/97)

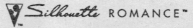

Silhouette ROMANCE™

As seen on TV!

Free Gift Offer

With a Free Gift proof-of-purchase from any Silhouette® book, you can receive **a** beautiful cubic zirconia pendant.

This gorgeous marquise-shaped stone is a genuine cubic zirconia—accented by an 18" gold tone necklace.

(Approximate retail value $19.95)

Send for yours today...

compliments of ▼ *Silhouette®*
™

To receive your free gift, a cubic zirconia pendant, send us one original proof-of-purchase, photocopies not accepted, from the back of any Silhouette Romance™, Silhouette Desire®, Silhouette Special Edition®, Silhouette Intimate Moments® or Silhouette Yours Truly™ title available in August, September, October, November and December at your favorite retail outlet, together with the Free Gift Certificate, plus a check or money order for $1.65 U.S./$2.15 CAN. (do not send cash) to cover postage and handling, payable to Silhouette Free Gift Offer. We will send you the specified gift. Allow 6 to 8 weeks for delivery. Offer good until December 31, 1996 or while quantities last. Offer valid in the U.S. and Canada only.

Free Gift Certificate

Name: _____

Address: _____

City: _____ State/Province: _____ Zip/Postal Code: _____

Mail this certificate, one proof-of-purchase and a check or money order for postage and handling to: SILHOUETTE FREE GIFT OFFER 1996. In the U.S.: 3010 Walden Avenue, P.O. Box 9077, Buffalo NY 14269-9077. In Canada: P.O. Box 613, Fort Erie, Ontario L2Z 5X3.

FREE GIFT OFFER   084-KMD

ONE PROOF-OF-PURCHASE

To collect your fabulous FREE GIFT, a cubic zirconia pendant, you must include this original proof-of-purchase for each gift with the properly completed Free Gift Certificate.

084-KMD-R

The collection of the year!
NEW YORK TIMES BESTSELLING AUTHORS

Linda Lael Miller
Wild About Harry

Janet Dailey
Sweet Promise

Elizabeth Lowell
Reckless Love

Penny Jordan
Love's Choices

and featuring
Nora Roberts
The Calhoun Women

This special trade-size edition features four of the wildly
popular titles in the Calhoun miniseries together in
one volume—a true collector's item!

Pick up these great authors and a chance to win
a weekend for two in New York City at the
Marriott Marquis Hotel on Broadway! We'll pay
for your flight, your hotel—even a Broadway show!

Available in December at your favorite retail outlet.

NEW YORK
Marriott®
MARQUIS

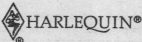 HARLEQUIN®  Silhouette®

NYT1296-R

Bundles of Joy

The biggest romantic surprises come in the smallest packages!

January:

HAVING GABRIEL'S BABY by Kristin Morgan (#1199)
After one night of passion Joelle was expecting! The dad-to-be, rancher Gabriel Lafleur, insisted on marriage. But could they find true love as a family?

April:

YOUR BABY OR MINE? by Marie Ferrarella (#1216)
Single daddy Alec Beckett needed help with his infant daughter! When the lovely Marissa Rogers took the job with an infant of her own, Alec realized he wanted this mom-for-hire *permanently*—as part of a real family!

Don't miss these irresistible Bundles of Joy, coming to you in January and April, only from

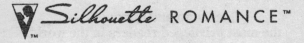

Silhouette ROMANCE™

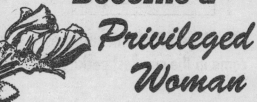

You're About to Become a *Privileged Woman*

Reap the rewards of fabulous free gifts and benefits with proofs-of-purchase from Silhouette and Harlequin books

Pages & Privileges™

It's our way of thanking you for buying our books at your favorite retail stores.

PROOF OF PURCHASE
SR-PP20
Offer expires March 31, 1997

Pages & Privileges ™

Harlequin and Silhouette— the most privileged readers in the world!

For more information about Harlequin and Silhouette's PAGES & PRIVILEGES program call the Pages & Privileges Benefits Desk: 1-503-794-2499

Silhouette®

SR-PP20